AMBUSH!

The seat of Windy's pants had no more than touched saddle leather when the first crashing explosion split the night silence. The angry red flame of muzzle flashes dotted the darkness, followed by the startled yells of men trying to control frightened mounts and return fire at the same time.

"They've been jumped in the draw, Matt," Mandalion said.

"Yeah. I heard Wojensky telling his men to fall back and form a firing line. They were taken completely by surprise. Come on, let's get our boys out of this. You circle around and take them from the north flank, I'll close in on the south and wait until you fire before I make my move."

"Good a plan as any. Happy huntin'," Windy said as he drove his heels against his horse's flanks and vanished...

EASY COMPANY

EASY COMPANY

AND THE INDIAN DOCTOR

JOHN WESLEY HOWARD

A JOVE BOOK

EASY COMPANY AND THE INDIAN DOCTOR

A Jove book/published by arrangement with
the author

PRINTING HISTORY
Jove edition / August 1982

ISBN: 0-515-06351-7

PRINTED IN THE UNITED STATES OF AMERICA

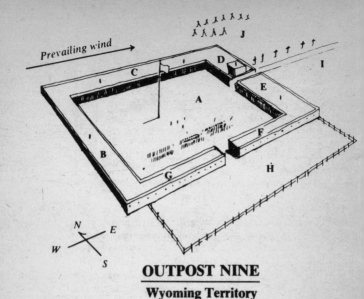

Prevailing wind

OUTPOST NINE

Wyoming Territory

KEY

A. Parade and flagstaff

B. Officers' quarters ("officers' country")

C. Enlisted men's quarters: barracks, day room, and mess

D. Kitchen, quartermaster supplies, ordnance shop, guardhouse

E. Suttler's store and other shops, tack room, and smithy

F. Stables

G. Quarters for dependents and guests; communal kitchen

H. Paddock

I. Road and telegraph line to regimental headquarters

J. Indian camp occupied by transient "friendlies"

OUTPOST NUMBER NINE
(DETAIL)

Outpost Number Nine is a typical High Plains military outpost of the days following the Battle of the Little Big Horn, and is the home of Easy Company. It is not a "fort"; an official fort is the headquarters of a regiment. However, it resembles a fort in its construction.

The birdseye view shows the general layout and orientation of Outpost Number Nine; features are explained in the Key.

The detail shows a cross-section through the outpost's double walls, which ingeniously combine the functions of fortification and shelter.

The walls are constructed of sod, dug from the prairie on which Outpost Number Nine stands, and are sturdy enough to withstand an assault by anything less than artillery. The roof is of log beams covered by planking, tarpaper, and a top layer of sod. It also provides a parapet from which the outpost's defenders can fire down on an attacking force.

one ═══════════════

Sergeant Gus Olsen, a burly, battle-scarred veteran of countless wars and lesser encounters on the Great Plains, wiped his eyes clear of water with the back of a sleeve and studied the empty, rolling plains behind him. A steady, drenching rain fell from the leaden sky above and his blue forage uniform clung to brawny shoulders as he twisted slightly to gain a better view from around the rock behind which he lay. An endless sea of grass rippled in shimmering waves on gusts of wind, and the apparent tranquility of the undulating swells extending to the horizon seemed to accent the universal silence. Where just minutes before the sodden air had been split by the crashing of gunfire, there was now a sullen calm, as though the storm itself had consumed the anger of men intent upon killing. The drumming hoofbeats of a running firefight had vanished from the plains as well, and the echoes of a brief, fierce battle had been swallowed by the timeless vastness of the prairie.

But there was one trace of the recent violence that the storm could not obliterate—the pinkish, water-diluted blood seeping between Olsen's fingers and spreading across the stomach of the man lying next to him, who was partially concealed by the low outcropping of rock. Mindless of the warmth turning cold beneath his palm, Olsen's eyes swept toward the narrow ravine before him, within which his attackers had taken refuge. The product of centuries of nature's labor, the ravine was perhaps twenty yards wide at the opening where it was carved between two abrupt swells, then narrowed as it curved to the left to rise sharply at the rear in what was a waterfall during the wet season. Olsen knew the surrounding terrain as well as did any white man in the area, and, in that knowledge, he was aware that his quarry had no escape via the opening facing him. He blinked the rain from his eyes, and the look on his face was one of grim determination, which softened only when he glanced down at the sound of a moan.

"How ya doin', Stoney?" he asked, raising his hand slightly to check the flow of blood from the compression bandage he held in place on the soldier's stomach. The crimson liquid oozed from the ragged, massive hole in the private's tunic with no lessening of flow, and Olsen knew his question had more to do with the soldier's comfort than with any hope of his survival.

The old soldier, nearly bald except for wisps of thinning hair plastered against his forehead, opened his eyes hesitantly, and the deeply set wrinkles around his mouth contorted in an effort to smile.

"Not so bad," he said softly, "for a drowning man."

"Hell, Stoney, ain't no little storm like this gonna get an old ball-buster like you. We'll get you back to the post and have you patched up in no time. Give that little scratch of yours a week or two, and you'll be back dancin' the jig before—"

The old soldier shook his head and his eyes lowered as he grimaced against the pain. "You can't bullshit an old bullshitter, Sarge, you know that. Old Stoney played a king and came up against an ace this hand. Don't be wastin' your time tryin' to take care of me." The eyes attempted to open, fluttered, then closed once again. "Just do me one favor, Sarge. One favor, one last time."

2

"Sure, Stoney," Olsen replied. "You name it."

"Get the bastards what did this to me. Get 'em good and leave 'em dead to rot in this godforsaken place. It'll make hell a mite easier for old Stoney if he knows he's gonna have some company."

Olsen's gaze drifted to the ravine once more, and a bitter hardness came into his eyes. "We'll get 'em, Stoney, don't worry about that. They're trapped, and with this storm they'll have to come out sooner or later. The rain won't be long in comin', and when it does, they'll either ride out, walk out, or float out. Don't matter which way they choose, 'cause there's seven Springfields waitin' to greet 'em."

Stoney Jenkins tried to chuckle, but coughed instead, and a flow of blood trickled from the corner of his mouth.

"Take it easy now, Stoney, damn you!" Olsen hissed, wiping the blood away with a corner of his neckerchief. "Don't try to talk. Don't do anything but lay there. Every time you move, the bleedin' starts up again."

Now the eyes opened and their slight twinkle was accentuated by the glaze of moisture. "Bleedin' ain't never gonna stop, Gus. I know that well as you. Ain't a mule in all of Tennessee what could kick as hard as that slug I took in the gut, and there ain't no piece of rag what's gonna fill up the hole, neither. My layin' here and takin' so damned long to die," he said weakly, "ain't helpin' nobody, an' I'm just holdin' you boys up. Kindly hand me my old Scoff layin' beside ya there, an' I'll—"

"Like hell you will!" Olsen snapped. He could feel the steady drizzle turn to a pelting rain across his back, and he knew a spring deluge with attendant flash floods was almost upon them. His left hand unconsciously pressed more tightly against Stoney's stomach while his eyes went again to the ravine. What had been glistening sand and pebbles minutes before was now a gurgling rivulet turned a dull brown with mud scoured from the creekbed. Olsen made a mental calculation: If the driving rain turned to a downpour, as he knew it would, in less than five minutes the narrow draw would be filled waist-high to a tall man with rushing water. He wiped the barrel of his revolver across his chest to clear moisture from the front sight, then carefully drew the hammer back.

"Sergeant?"

"Yeah, Miller?" Olsen replied, recognizing the voice of

Corporal Miller, his squad leader, coming from somewhere behind him and to the left.

"Should be comin' out any minute, Sarge."

"Yeah, I know. Your boys ready?"

"They are. Three on the far bank and four over here."

"Good. They've been told to hold their fire?"

"Didn't have to tell 'em," Miller replied tersely. "This ain't their first time out behind the shithouse, Sarge. How's Stoney doin'?"

"He's a tough old bastard, but—" Olsen looked down at the ashen-faced man stretched out in the grass, and he saw vacant eyes staring straight up, awash with rain and unblinking. The wispy gray hair had parted and dropped across the sides of his forehead like an old mop discarded over a porch railing. His mouth, slightly agape, had also filled with water, which dribbled down his chin. Olsen's head lowered for a second, as though a heavy weariness had suddenly swept over him, then he reached out with his gun hand and closed the eyelids gently with the tip of a thumb. "But not tough enough, I guess," he concluded, wiping his bloody left hand on his pants leg. "He's dead."

"Poor old son of a bitch," Miller mumbled, his lowered voice muted even more by the storm. "Used to be a sergeant, didn't he?"

"Yeah. Till the whiskey got to him. We rode together during the War."

"Any family?"

"Naw. Just the goddamned army, like the rest of us, I 'spect. Good old feller he was, but that don't put no apples back on the tree."

The rushing flow of the stream was now nearly a foot deep and rising fast, and Olsen wondered fleetingly if his prey could have escaped through the rear of the draw. Then he rejected the thought, leveled his Scoff over the rock, and waited, counting the minutes and watching the water swell beyond the streambed and begin to lap the leading edge of the grass.

Suddenly he heard a defiant scream mixed with the splash of hooves pounding through water, and the first horse broke around the bend with a rider bent low to its withers and firing blindly to the front. Olsen calmly shot the mount through the neck, chambered another round as he watched the half-breed catapult over his horse's head, then fired at the man struggling

4

to regain his footing in the swirling water. The slug slammed into the renegade and he sprawled backward with a massive hole in his chest. The reddish gush of blood was quickly lost to the muddy flow.

Olsen's first shot had accomplished its intended purpose, and now the fallen horse partially blocked the narrow channel. The two horses following closely behind reared, spun on flailing hooves, then leaped over the dead animal and into the withering fire of the first squad of Olsen's First Platoon. Both horses went down, their riders dead before they hit the ground, while a fourth horse managed to clear the jumbled mass of flesh and raced down the streambed. Its rider, slightly built and light upon the horse's back, provided little weight and the mount was nearly free of the ravine and onto the open prairie when Olsen thumbed his final round home, took careful aim, and sent the rider sprawling face-first into the mud.

The echo of shots quickly vanished from the death scene and a heavy silence swallowed up the sounds of battle. Olsen waited for nearly a minute while reloading his Scoff, his eyes never leaving the mouth of the ravine as his fingers artfully manipulated the heavy brass cartridges.

"How many'd you count goin' in there, Miller?" he asked, almost matter-of-factly. "I made it to be four."

"Same here, Sarge. And I count four dead ones down there."

"Maybe," Olsen replied cautiously. "Take one man, follow the high ground, and check the back end of that ravine. I'll take one with me down to check for dead and wounded. The other three can cover us from up here."

"Right, Sarge. Canfield! Come with me! Owens! Go with the sergeant! The rest of you keep a tight ass and a sharp eye!"

With Owens waiting on the bank and keeping his weapon trained on the stilled forms lying sprawled in the stream, Olsen waded into the swollen water and examined each body individually. He didn't recognize any of the three, one white man and two half-breeds, and none carried any identification. Their saddlebags revealed nothing of their past, and each horse had been branded with a different iron. Before quitting the stream and turning toward the fourth man, Olsen pulled his Schofield model Smith & Wesson from its holster and mercifully put a single bullet through the head of a horse struggling to rise on a broken leg. Then he splashed along the streambed to where the fourth body lay motionless, with rising water now lapping

5

at a pair of surprisingly small boots. In comparison to the others, it was a diminutive figure, and he wondered if he had accidentally shot a young boy. Clothed in a heavy, baggy coat and oversized pants, and with a hat pulled well down over the ears, the body resembled something that might have been discarded with unwanted rags. He could see a splotch of blood behind the left shoulder where his bullet had entered, and judging from the point of entry, it didn't appear that the shot could have hit any vital organs. A flash of hope touched his mind and he knelt down quickly to listen for breathing and a heartbeat. Hearing nothing, he pressed his ear more tightly against the frail back while drawing a narrow hand from beneath the body to check for a pulse. He heard shallow, ragged breathing and could feel the sluggish pumping of blood through the right hand. He jerked the kerchief from around his neck, formed it into a loose wad, and stuffed it down the boy's jacket to plug the hole in his shoulder, then turned him gently onto his side.

Even through the thick coating of mud on the young man's face, Olsen could make out the finely chiseled features, light facial structure, and high cheekbones of a boy not yet old enough to shave, yet apparently old enough to ride with a band of renegades. Feeling a mixture of pity and contempt sweep through him, he rose and turned toward Owens.

"Private! This one's alive. Get a horse over here fast, and if we can get him back to the post in time, maybe we can save him! Might be able to give us some answers we'll never get with him dead!"

"Yes, Sergeant!" Owens replied, turning to claw and crawl his way up the slippery bank.

When the soldier returned with a mount, Olsen lifted the slight body in his arms, lay it over the saddle, strapped it down with a picket rope, and led the horse back to the crest. By the time they had Stoney Jenkins draped facedown across his mount, Corporal Miller had returned with three branding irons in his hand.

"Found these in the draw," Miller said. "Must've wanted to get rid of the extra weight when they made a break for it."

Olsen turned the irons in his hand while examining them. "Looks like it. Probably figured to use this storm to hide their tracks. Let's get back to the post and see what Lieutenant Kincaid makes of all this." He nodded toward the unconscious form, which seemed even more pitiful now in its ragged clothing and further drenched by the lashing storm. "If things are as they appear, we just might be able to save one for the hangman's noose. Mount the squad, and let's go. One of the men will have to ride double behind that little asshole over there."

The two men standing beneath the awning attached to the orderly-room section of Outpost Number Nine ceased their conversation at a snapping crackle of lightning, and waited for the rolling peal of thunder, which was a mere four seconds in coming. The heavy downpour of rain sloshed over the sides of the cut-pole barrier and made a drumming tattoo on the packed earth of the parade. Referred to as a "soddy" in deference to its sod-and-cut-lumber construction, Outpost Number Nine was one of a few far-flung fortresses built by the United States government to give a representation of military presence on the High Plains of Wyoming Territory. Rectangular in construction, with a flagpole erected in the center of the parade, it was designed more for a utilitarian purpose than as a haven of creature comforts for those assigned there. In the summertime, dust and flies were an ever-present nuisance, and during the winter the quarters leaked muddy water and were often drafty.

But even with the restraints of their spartan existence, the unit assigned there, Easy Company, a detachment of mounted infantry, was the exemplification of a breed of hard, durable men and women who had been assigned to a particular mission and who had no intention of allowing either hardship or self-deprivation to stand in the way of their given task. Frontier duty was known in army circles to be tough, often miserable, and always unforgiving of those uninitiated to the will and whimsy of the vast High Plains country.

The two officers who stood side by side while waiting for the thunderclap to be sucked back into the blackness were uniquely similar in some ways and distinctly different in others. Each was dressed in a dark blue uniform with light blue piping, and the carriage of both was that of men born to command.

On the right was Captain Warner Conway, commanding officer of Outpost Number Nine, and a striking figure of a man. Tall, broad-shouldered, and slightly graying at the temples, Conway was a Virginian by birth, but had fought under General Grant during the Civil War. His rank should have been that of major, but due to the isolation and obscurity of his post, he had been passed over by the promotions board several times, and even though he had attained the rank of lieutenant colonel during the war, there was no visible bitterness about him regarding his current status as a captain. Without doubt, Conway would have liked to be promoted, but he accepted the status quo and directed his energies toward the welfare of the men under his command. As it was, he had more than ample difficulty getting his men paid on time, properly equipped, and adequately supplied, securing promotions due, and attempting to get competent replacements for soldiers who had died or been wounded in battle. He could endure the injustices of army life that had personally fallen his way, but he would brook no malfeasance when it came to the men of his command.

Standing beside the captain as they stared into the murky gloom was First Lieutenant Matt Kincaid, the executive officer and second-in-command of Easy Company. He was perhaps ten years younger than Conway, equally broad of shoulder, matching his commanding officer in height, and was graced with a slim posture and erect military bearing. There was a glitter about his gray eyes, as though he were more bemused than bitter about his having been passed over for promotion just as the captain had been, and there was a fullness to his hair that indicated a man in the prime of his life. Kincaid, a Connecticut Yankee, was a regular-army man, graduate of West Point, class of '69, and was now serving his second tour of duty on the frontier. He had been too late for the Civil War, but his military record showed a citation for bravery on the Staked Plains in the campaign against the Comanche.

Conway folded his hands behind his back and gave the cigar clenched between his teeth several testing puffs before accepting the fact that it had gone out, then glanced across at Kincaid.

"Damned poor weather for a night patrol, wouldn't you say, Matt?"

"Yes, it is, sir. But Olsen's detail was not intended to go beyond dusk. Unless he ran into trouble, he should have been back long before this."

"Trouble," Conway mused. "Gets to be a way of life, doesn't it?"

"Guess that's why we're here, sir."

"I suppose so, but a man wonders sometimes if the pathway

8

to hell isn't beaten by the footsteps of the well-intentioned. Here we are, trying our damnedest to supply the beef that was promised the Sioux in the treaties they signed, and the minute a few head get here, some son of a bitch decides to steal them. Of course, if we can't stop it, we're the ones who'll have to answer to Kills Many Bear, not the Bureau of Indian Affairs or the Interior Department."

"That's certainly true, sir. I guess they figure we're here to keep the Indians they've cheated and lied to from forming up a war party and invading Washington, but they must not think there's too much danger of that, or you can bet they'd give us more support."

Conway only grunted in reply, and the two men fell silent for a moment and listened to the rolling of thunder over the plains, then Kincaid said, "Oh, by the way, sir, about Stoney Jenkins . . ."

"What about him?"

"He's going to want to reenlist, sir, you know that."

"I know."

"His hitch is up in two weeks. I've read Olsen's field report on him, and it's his opinion that Stoney is a hazard while on patrol not only to himself, but to the remainder of the squad as well. Not that he doesn't try," Kincaid added quickly. "It's just that he's too damned old for combat patrol anymore. He's ridden for every army in every war he could find, and I guess the years are finally catching up to him."

Conway remained silent for several seconds, weighing Kincaid's remarks and seeking the hidden meaning that he had come to expect of his second-in-command. Finally he struck a match against the heel of his boot and touched flame to tobacco.

"I'm aware of that. That's why I've recommended his discharge. Seems to be the best solution for everyone concerned."

"True, perhaps, but not for the one man most concerned. Private Jenkins."

"How do you mean?" Conway asked, knowing his perceptions had not failed him. "There doesn't seem to be much else we can do."

"I think there is, sir. The army is Stoney's life, and he's known nothing else. It doesn't seem right to turn him out when his usefulness to us has ended. A good horse goes to stud, then to pasture, when his time in the mounted ranks is finished.

can't see why the same couldn't be done with a good and deserving soldier."

Conway squinted through a cloud of bluish smoke. "What are you getting at, Matt?"

"There are plenty of things that a man could do around the post without standing muster every morning. Stablehand, cook's helper, general handyman, instructor for new recruits, you name it. Why couldn't we allow Stoney to reenlist, give him a purpose in life, and keep him on the payroll? He's got more knowledge and experience as a soldier than you and I do put together, and it seems a damned shame to waste it."

Conway clasped his hands behind his back again and pursed his lips in thought. "Sounds logical, but unfortunately the top brass don't deal in logic. There is a directive, which I am sure you're well aware of, that specifically states that a man will be automatically retired once he reaches an age that renders him incapable for combat duty. I'm afraid Stoney has reached that age and then some. He was allowed to go on this last patrol, as you recall, only as a personal favor."

Kincaid nodded. "Yes, I realize that, sir. I think he knew the handwriting was on the wall and it was important for him to go on this one. But, as regards that directive, yes, I am familiar with it. I am equally as aware that you and I have read between the lines in the past and haven't been tripped up yet. It could well be that this post survives as a positive military presence precisely because we have taken the initiative to interpret the rules as they might best apply to the specific case at hand."

"We've certainly done that," Conway agreed with a chuckle. "Any commander who allows himself to be hogtied to some of those ridiculous ARs might just as well pack it in and take up homesteading."

"Exactly my point. That directive regarding the mandatory retirement age is not specific in terms of chronological years, is it, sir?"

"Hell, no. We don't know the exact age of half the men on post, and I don't think some of those same men do, either. What are you getting at, Matt?"

"Well, sir, all of that being true, the date that a man is no longer effective as a soldier, thus incurring mandatory retirement, seems to be entirely up to the commanding officer's judgment, and that of his subordinates. If Stoney were allowed to reenlist, only you and I would know he is no longer capable of combat patrol. As far as we're concerned, it isn't that he *can't* do it, but we just don't *assign* him to do it. His skills are more greatly needed in other areas of service."

Conway listened intently to Kincaid's slow, emphatic tone, and a grin gradually spread across his face. "By God, I think you're on to something, Matt," he said, laying a hand on Kincaid's shoulder. "There's always something in need of doing around here. But do you think old Stoney will mind doing lackey work? He's wearing a hatful of pride, that man."

"No, I don't, sir. Not if he's made to feel that what he's doing is important and that he's the best man for the job. We'll get on his ass every now and then so he won't be any different than anyone else in the command, and as long as he can wear his uniform, make the occasional trip outside the post, and such, I think he'll be entirely pleased with the arrangement. Besides, he won't know any arrangement has been made. He'll just be following orders."

"Fine," Conway said, clapping Matt's shoulder. "Consider it done. When he gets back from this patrol, present him with his reenlistment papers. Speaking of the patrol," the captain continued, his attention given once again to the stormy night, "if they aren't back by dawn, have a second squad ready to leave. It's not like Olsen to be this late."

"The second squad of First Platoon is standing by now, sir. They'll leave at first light if necessary."

Conway turned away with a wink. "Always one step ahead of me, aren't you, Matt? I like that. Now I think I'll mosey on over to my quarters and see what's for supper. Flora mentioned stew and biscuits this morning. Sounds kind of good on a night like this. Care to join us?"

"No, thanks, Captain, but I appreciate the offer just the same. Give my regards to Mrs. Conway. Night, sir."

"Good night, Matt," Conway replied, stepping into the storm while tugging his hat brim down with one hand to secure it against the gusting wind.

Kincaid watched the commanding officer depart as another flash of lightning seared the horizon with a sizzling streak of blue and briefly illuminating the parade. Then the captain was lost again in the blackness until a rectangle of warm yellow light appeared along the dark wall of officers' country. He hesitated momentarily, bathed in the yellow glow, then was stolen from the raging storm.

Kincaid adjusted his hat, pulled his coat forward to shield

11

his Scoff from wetness, then stepped out onto the parade and picked his way through the puddles as he angled toward the enlisted men's mess. He knew there would be hot coffee on the stove for the night guards coming off the walls after their four-hour round of sentry duty, and a steaming cup of that black brew was a pleasant thought to his mind. Besides, it would be a good place to wait out the night, as he always did when one of his squads was late in returning from patrol.

Just as he was about to step beneath the sheltering awning before the mess hall, another bolt of lightning crackled, and in between that sharp snap and the brief lull before a peal of thunder, he heard the sentry's call from his post near the main gate:

"Sergeant of the guard! Patrol comin' in!"

Thunder rolled, and then came the sergeant's reply: "Challenge!"

Another pause, then: "What's the password?"

"Potomac!"

"Open the gates!"

Instantly recognizing Olsen's voice, Kincaid angled toward the main gate, mindless now of the water trickling down his spine and slowly seeping into his boots. He had detected weariness and dejection in the sergeant's single spoken word, something beyond mere fatigue.

By the time he reached the gate, the squad was already filing in and Kincaid instantly saw the first empty saddle with a body lashed to it and a pair of black boots gleaming with a wet-slick shine in the weak light. He advanced to stand beside Olsen's horse, and returned the sergeant's salute before leaning a hand against the animal's withers.

"Glad to see you made it back, Sergeant."

"Glad to be back, sir."

Kincaid hesitated before nodding toward the riderless mount. "Who is it?"

"Stoney, sir. Took one full in the gut. Died about five hours ago."

"Damn!" Matt said almost under his breath. Then his eyes adjusted and he saw the second horse with a body tied across its back as well. "How many did you lose?"

"Just one, sir. That other feller's one of theirs. Just a kid, I think, but it was gettin' dark and he was all covered with mud, so I couldn't tell real well. I think he might live, looks like a bullet through the shoulder."

"What did you run up against?" Kincaid asked, shielding his eyes from the downpour and looking up at Olsen.

"Rustlers, just like you thought, sir. Kind of took us by surprise, though. That one back there's the only one left alive."

"Well, let's get out of this storm and then tell me about it. Have your men take care of their mounts, then tell them there'll be hot coffee and grub waiting in the mess hall for them. I'll get one of Dutch's boys to rustle something up." Kincaid hesitated as his eyes fell upon the old soldier who had just completed his last patrol. "Lay Stoney out in the stable and post an honorary guard over him tonight. I know it's nothing more than window dressing, but I think it'd mean a lot to him if he knew we cared that much. Meet me in the mess hall in fifteen minutes."

"Right, sir. And about Stoney—thank you, Lieutenant."

Kincaid didn't reply as he moved along the line to the wounded civilian, glanced at him for a second, then called to the bachelor officers' quarters, which was often utilized as a makeshift dispensary. After the injured man had been taken away, Matt stepped toward the noncoms' billet, and rapped his knuckles on the quarters of Dutch Rothausen, the mess sergeant and sometime doctor in the absence of professional medical help. Fat, easily irritated, and always grouchy, even during the best of times, Rothausen was less than polite upon being awakened during the middle of the night.

"Get away from that door, goddammit!" a moderately sleepy and throughly irate voice growled from within. "If I open that sonofabitch and find a fuckin' KP standin' out there, we'll have his balls for breakfast in the mornin'!"

Kincaid couldn't help but smile as his fist went to the door again. "Sergeant! This is Lieutenant Kincaid. Get up. I need your help."

A bed groaned, boots scraped the floor, then the door opened and a red-faced sergeant stood there in his woolen underwear while attempting to drag on his pants.

"Beggin' your pardon, Lieutenant. Thought it was some lazy-assed KP come to tell me he had a bellyache or some damned thing. Didn't know it was you."

"I assumed as much, Sergeant. Sorry to drag you out like this, but we've got a wounded civilian who needs some attention. Bullet through the shoulder, Olsen says."

13

"Serves a goddamned civilian right for gettin' in the way in the first place," Rothausen mumbled sullenly as he pulled up his suspenders. "Should let the sonofabitch die just on principle alone."

"Can't do that, Dutch," Kincaid said almost gently. "If we can save him, he might be just what we need to stop the theft of government beef."

"Government beef?" Rothausen scoffed, dragging a soiled white apron around his waist. "Anybody dumb enough to go out of their way to steal that tough, gristly shit deserves what they get. Be right there, Lieutenant, soon as I find my hat."

Kincaid had just poured two cups of coffee and sat down at a table when Sergeant Olsen stepped into the mess hall and eased down on a bench. After Olsen had eagerly drunk the entire cup of coffee, Kincaid refilled the mug and shoved it across to the sergeant.

"What happened, Gus?"

"Well, we went to the agency like you said, sir, and talked with old Roy Stearns, the agent. He said he thought some of his beef had been trailed off. We took a little look-see around and couldn't really find nothin' and were headed back this way when we crossed the trail of about thirty head being pushed south. It had started to rain when we caught up with 'em about an hour before dusk. They weren't in any hurry, and nothing looked suspicious, so I kind of took 'em for a regular bunch of cowhands tryin' to get their stock in before the storm. There were four of 'em, and they saw us about the same time we saw them, so the leader rode out to meet us about a hundred yards from the herd."

Olsen shook his head and stared moodily into the cup. "Seemed like a friendly sort. He mentioned the coming storm, the need to get his cattle in and all that, and said he was foreman for the Standing Y. I told him that was fine by me, but that I had been ordered to check the brands on all cattle being moved in that area and he said I was welcome to go ahead. Matter of fact, he said he'd take us around the herd, so me and Stoney went with him and I left the rest of the detachment behind to keep an eye on the other three. Dumbest thing I ever did, I guess," Olsen concluded, his voice trailing off. "Takin' Stoney with me, I mean."

Kincaid waited a moment before saying, "Sounds to me like you did everything according to regulations, Gus. What happened after that?"

14

"Well, I guess Stoney saw it before me, and I owe him my life 'cause of it. When we got close to the rear of the herd, with the two of us ridin' just behind that dirty bastard, he turns in his saddle like he's gonna say something. At the same time his hand went to his revolver, which I couldn't see 'cause of the angle and all. Just as his gun cleared leather, he fired. Old Stoney had moved his mount forward, which put him between me and the bullet. He took it in the stomach, and the rest you know." Olsen turned the cup silently in his fingertips before adding, "It was kind of like maybe he wanted to go out that way."

"Maybe so, Gus. Maybe so. Old-timers like him seem to think different than the new breed. What happened after that?

"It happened real fast and took me by surprise, to say the least," the sergeant began again, shaking his head slowly as he recalled the events of the afternoon. "The impact of the slug threw Stoney backward across my horse's neck while at the same time that sonofabitchin' rustler took off like a streak of greased owlshit. But the time I got my weapon out and took aim, him and his partners were out of range. I sent the squad after 'em, then got Stoney back in his saddle and we brought up the rear. They must not have known the lay of the land very well—which tells me they weren't local—'cause they headed into Alder's Ravine, where my boys cornered them. There ain't any way out the backside, and it was just a matter of waiting for 'em to make their move. When they did, we took 'em. Three dead and one wounded.

"Well, let's hope old Dutch can save that wounded man. I think this operation is bigger than four people could handle, and I'd like to find out who else is involved." Kincaid downed the last of his coffee and watched Olsen closely as he lowered his cup. "Don't take it too hard about Stoney, Gus. He was a bit rough around the edges sometimes, but he was a good soldier. He did what he did because he wanted to, not because he had to. Tomorrow we'll give him a burial with full military honors. He doesn't deserve anything less."

"Thanks, Lieutenant. I'd kinda like to say a few words over him when we do, if you don't mind."

"Not at all. I thought you might want to do that." Kincaid laid his palms on the table and started to rise. "Get some sleep now and—"

"Lieutenant?"

Matt turned to see Dutch Rothausen standing in the doorway

with an obviously puzzled look on his face.

"Yes, Sergeant? What is it?"

"First off, that civilian of yours is gonna need better medical help than I can give. Bullet's lodged up under the collarbone, and somebody's gonna have to operate before the fever sets in too bad."

"All right. We'll see if we can't get the doctor out from town tomorrow. Do the best you can for him until then. You said 'first off.' Is there something else?"

Rothausen scratched the stubble along his jowls with digging strokes of his thick, blunt fingers as he contemplated how to phrase what he would say next. "Yeah, there is, sir. He ain't a *him*, Lieutenant."

"What?"

"That's right, sir. You done got yourself a woman prisoner, not a man."

"Are you sure?" Kincaid asked incredulously.

Rothausen grinned sheepishly. "I'll admit it's been a long time 'tween looks, Lieutenant, but if that's a man you've got back there, he's got the nicest set of tits I ever did see." The tinge of red creeping into the gruff sergeant's cheeks might have indicated the beginnings of a blush, and he spoke rapidly with some embarrassment to clarify his remark. "What I mean is, I wasn't tryin' for no cheap peeks or anything. I thought it was a man, like you said, and to treat his wound I took his— uh, I mean, *her* shirt off like I would anybody else's. There they was, starin' at me like two eggs sunny side up on a plate. Then I took her hat off and she had hair stacked up inside that'd most likely reach clear down to the crack of her ass. When I washed the mud caked on her face away, it was a woman all right, pretty as you please."

"Well, I'll be damned!" Kincaid exclaimed. "How old would you make her out to be?"

"Twenty, maybe twenty-two," Rothausen answered with a shrug.

"Is she conscious?"

"No. I suspicion she's runnin' a pretty high fever, what with the infection and all. She keeps mumbling about some feller named Slater, whoever in hell he is, and it sounds like she's almighty scared of him. I can't make heads or tails of it myself. Care to have a look with your own eyes, Lieutenant? She'd make a mighty pretty woman if she was dressed up like a lady

16

'stead of some damned saddle tramp." Rothausen started to turn in the doorway, then stopped. "Kinda hated to do it, but I covered her tits up again. Didn't seem quite right to have people lookin' at 'em with her unconscious and all."

"You did the right thing, Sergeant." Kincaid replied, concealing the hint of a smile tugging at the corners of his mouth at the thought of the tough old sergeant being tender and compassionate toward anyone. "I'm going to talk with the captain right now, and maybe he can have Mrs. Conway find some proper clothes for her. Keep an eye on her through the night for me. Maybe she's got the answers to some questions."

Then he paused and looked away. "As it stands right now, she's got cattle stealing and a murder charge hanging over her head."

two ─────────────────────

"What do you make of it, Captain?" Kincaid asked as the two officers looked down at the exceptionally pretty young woman stretched out on the cot. "She doesn't exactly look like your usual cow thief."

"No, she doesn't," Conway agreed, "but we've got to keep in mind that Gus didn't shoot her on her way to choir practice either."

With her auburn hair now combed free of tangles, the result of Flora's gentle brushing, and wearing a pink nightgown with white lace trimming, which the captain's lady had donated, she was the picture of tranquil beauty; her shallow breathing was the only sign of life about her. Her deeply tanned skin was smooth and free of blemishes, and there was a delicate look about her full lips, which, in another setting, might have indicated a passionate, sensual woman. Long lashes rested peacefully on sculptured cheeks, and during one brief moment of delirium, her wide hazel eyes had filled with imagined horror and then faded to opaque blankness once again.

Flora Conway looked up from dabbing a cool, damp cloth around the young woman's forehead, and Kincaid noticed, as he had on other occasions, that she was equally as beautiful when angry as she was when being her normally cheerful self. "You men," she said contemptuously. "Always suspicious. Would it be asking too much of your self-restraint to wait until she has recovered enough to defend herself before you slip a noose around her neck? Just because she was with those men doesn't mean she *wanted* to be with them." Flora took the cloth away momentarily and gazed down at the young woman. "I just can't believe this woman could be a cattle thief and guilty of murder. I just can't believe that."

"I don't believe Private Jenkins would have believed it either, my dear," Conway said in what was intended to be a consoling tone but which had a definitely incriminating ring about it. "He's dead and she's alive; that's got to tell you something."

"Alive, yes. But barely. Where is that doctor from town?"

"I sent a man in this morning to bring him out, and he should be here anytime. She shouldn't be moved until then, and all we can do is wait until the doctor arrives. The way it looks, old Dutch has got the bleeding stopped pretty well, and I'd hate to see that wound opened again."

Flora shook her head in helpless dismay. "Is that out of concern for a human life, Warner, or because you're afraid you might lose a witness to the crime?" Immediately she knew she had said the wrong thing, and she reached out to lay a hand gently on her husband's arm. "I'm sorry, dear. I didn't mean that the way it sounded. I know you're just as concerned about her welfare as I am, and your legal concerns are entirely justified. It's just that . . . she looks so helpless and innocent lying there."

Conway cleared his throat and his tightened grip relaxed on the hat brim in his hand. "The question of guilt or innocence is to be decided by a magistrate of the territory, Flora, and her fate is entirely in the hands of God, neither of whom I pretend to be. Until such time as a decision is passed down by one of those two powers, she is to be considered a prisoner, no matter how innocent and peaceful she may appear to be. I don't mean

20

to sound overly firm, but that's the way things stand. Thank you for your concern just the same," he concluded, smiling tightly and patting her hand before turning to Kincaid.

"The services for Private Jenkins should be about ready to start, Matt. I think we'd best be going." Again he looked at Flora. "Will you stay here with her, Flora, and give her whatever comfort you can until the doctor arrives?"

"Of course. What's happening to her, and what has happened, must be a terrifying thing. Maggie will be by shortly to help as well."

Just as Conway and Kincaid stepped outside, Maggie Cohen came bustling toward them with the handle of a filled water bucket grasped in either strong hand.

"Morning, Mrs. Cohen," Matt said politely, tipping his hat.

"Good morning to you, Lieutenant. Would you be having nothing better to do than stand around gawking at a lady in distress?" she asked, brushing by Kincaid and glancing briefly at Conway. "A good morning to you too, Captain. I trust your beautiful wife is tending to the injured girl?"

"That she is, Maggie, and good morning. Flora's expecting you, as a matter of fact. Thanks for stopping by."

"I wouldn't be just 'stopping by' with a bucket of water in either hand, now would I, Captain?" Maggie asked with an unmistakable mischievous twinkle in her green eyes. "Unless, of course, I'm looked upon as a stablehand now."

"Of course not, Maggie. What I meant was—"

Mrs. Cohen laughed heartily, dismissing the officers as she stepped through the doorway.

Kincaid and the captain walked side by side across the parade in the general direction of the main gate, and Matt chuckled as he adjusted his hat on his head. "One of a kind, isn't she, Captain? The rose and the thorn wrapped into one."

"She certainly is," Conway agreed. "She's the kind of woman who would keep most bachelors like yourself single, and most married men like Ben Cohen in the traces. The lioness and the lamb both at the same time."

With the exception of the sentries manning their posts, the entire company had been assembled in dress uniform near Private Jenkins's gravesite, and even with their somewhat frayed appearance, they presented the solemn appearance of a proud fighting unit standing ranks for the last time in honor of a fallen comrade. Even though death was not an uncommon thing to the soldiers of Easy Company, there had been a special quality about Stoney Jenkins that had made him unique among the ranks. It might have been his age and accumulated years of survival in the arduous business of soldiering, but it was more likely his spirit and never-say-die attitude. Even in his advancing years, he had never asked for less than his full share of responsibility, whether that meant digging latrines or shivering through long nights of guard duty with the temperature dipping below the freezing mark. He never bemoaned his existence as nothing more than a common soldier, which was relatively simple for him, because he didn't consider soldiers, good soldiers, to be common. To Stoney Jenkins, they were a breed apart. Now he lay cold and stiff in a simple, flag-draped coffin situated near a yawning grave.

"Company assembled and prepared for the services, Captain," Sergeant Ben Cohen said as the two officers approached. The three men matched smart salutes, then Cohen stepped forward and continued in a lowered voice, "We'll keep it short and sweet like you said, sir. I'm in complete agreement with you, Captain. Stoney wasn't a man much given to long speeches, and he wouldn't want a whole bunch of patriotic and religious drivel spilled across his grave. A quart of good whiskey maybe, but none of the other."

"I doubt that he would have liked that, either, Ben," Conway replied, glancing briefly at the coffin. "He'd be throughly irate at the sight of good whiskey being poured on the ground. Let's get on with it."

Conway looked up as a buckboard, drawn by a lone horse, topped a distant swell. He recognized the silhouette of the slouch-shouldered man perched on the seat, holding the reins limply in total disinterest. He had met Dr. Amos Barkley numerous times during his years at Outpost Number Nine, and had never developed a liking for the man. With his ever-present cigar clenched beneath a nicotine-stained, yellow-gray moustache, he was a man of little apparent humor who was given more to grunting his way through a conversation than actively engaging in one. And while he seemed a competent physician, there was often an air of detachment about his work, as though he were a tradesman engaged in the repair of some inanimate object rather than a human being holding the life and welfare of another human being in the grip of his hands and the grasp of his knowledge.

Conway had decided long ago to keep his communication and involvement with the doctor to the barest minimum, but that decision went beyond mere mutual dislike. His unspoken enmity was founded in the belief that the doctor held the lives of soldiers wounded in battle in even more contempt than he did that of civilians—an unforgivable transgression, to Conway's way of thinking.

Feeling the contempt build, Conway turned toward Kincaid and said dryly, "It looks like the doctor is proceeding at his customary breakneck pace, Matt. Ride out and meet him, will you? Tell him what we've got and then come back here. We'll hold up the ceremony for you."

"Yes, sir," Kincaid replied, lifting his reins to turn his horse, then stopping. "Now who the hell is that?" he asked, pointing a gloved hand in the direction of the wagon.

Conway's eyes again went in the direction indicated, and he saw a lone soldier maintaining what appeared to be a comfortable distance between himself and the cantankerous old medical man, while riding perhaps twenty yards behind the buckboard.

"Beats hell out of me," Conway said, studying the tall, lean frame clothed in a uniform of such brilliant hue that it might well have just come from the quartermaster's shelf. "We weren't expecting any replacements, were we?" he asked in a puzzled tone.

"Not that I know of, sir. What do you make of it?"

"I'm not quite sure. Guess we'll know soon enough. Check him out when you talk to the doctor."

"Yes, sir," Kincaid said, touching his hat brim in a light salute and moving his mount forward at an easy gallop. The captain watched as Kincaid's horse came abreast of the buckboard, which continued in its plodding pace without pausing. He saw Matt lean down and say something to the doctor, pointing toward the BOQ, and he noted Barkley's nod. Kincaid shrugged as the buckboard moved away, and turned to await the approach of the unannounced officer. There was a momentary conversaton, an exchange of salutes, a brief handshake, and then both mounts cantered toward where the captain was waiting. Conway thought he noted a sly, knowing grin on Kincaid's face as he pushed his sweat-stained hat back slightly and indicated the man beside him with a wave of his other hand.

23

"Captain Conway, Lieutenant Fred Morris. Lieutenant? This is the commanding officer of Outpost Number Nine, Captain Warner Conway."

Conway's eyes swept over the young man before him as salutes were exchanged. He estimated the sandy-haired second lieutenant at somewhere near twenty-five years of age. Even though there was a bright look in his eyes, Lieutenant Morris had a sallow look about him, and while he was not exactly skinny, there was a certain frailness to his features, despite the shoulders thrown back in correct military posture.

"Nice to meet you, Lieutenant," Conway offered cordially. "What brings you to Outpost Number Nine?"

Morris couldn't contain a furtive glance at the rough-hewn, isolated fortress situated some hundred yards to the left. "Is this Outpost Number Nine, sir?" he asked, mindless of the incredulousness in his voice.

"In all its splendor, Lieutenant," Conway said with a wink at Kincaid. "You were expecting something a little more glamorous, perhaps?"

Morris's face reddened. "No, sir . . . not at all. I . . . I just thought—"

"That maybe you'd taken a wrong turn somewhere around Omaha? You didn't. If you were looking for Outpost Number Nine, Wyoming Territory, you just found it. What brings you here? I don't remember being informed of any officers being sent as replacements."

Kincaid rose in his stirrups, shifted in his saddle. "He isn't a replacement, sir. He's a doctor."

"A what?"

"A doctor, sir," Morris said hastily, reaching toward the inside breast pocket of his tunic, which still bore traces of folds from a shipping container. "I have my orders right here, Captain."

Conway waved the gesture aside. "Lieutenant Kincaid will have a look at them later. We could use a regular doctor around here, but I thought we were too small a post to rate one." Then he added wryly, "I was given to understand that most of the dead and wounded around here were to be found behind desks at regimental headquarters."

"I don't understand it either, sir," Morris agreed, thoroughly confused. "But my orders clearly state—"

"I'm sure they do," Conway broke in. "But we've received

artillery gun wadding instead of requested small-arms ammunition before, so your arrival here is no real surprise." Conway's eyes swept over the waiting company. "We'll look into your dilemma later, but right now we've got a soldier to bury who might be alive if we'd had a man of your training assigned here before." Now the captain eyed the young officer closely. "He was gutshot at close range. Damned near tore his entire stomach out. Ever worked on anything like that before, Doctor?"

"Ah . . . no . . . can't say I have, sir. I was commissioned the day after I graduated from the University of Pennsylvania, Captain. That was two months ago." Morris glanced uncomfortably at the plain wooden box within which rested the remains of Private Jenkins, and cleared his throat self-consciously. "The only dead men I've seen were cadavers supplied to the university by the Philadelphia morgue, and I've never worked on a live wounded man in my life."

"I admire your honesty and candor," Conway said with a nod. "Give yourself about two weeks with us, and that won't be the case anymore. And we supply our own dead and wounded," he concluded grimly, while glancing at Kincaid. "Let's get it over with, Matt. Then maybe Lieutenant Morris here can help old Doc Barkley with the girl. Might as well get his feet wet, so to speak."

"Do you already have a doctor here, sir?" Morris asked in surprise.

"No. He's on loan to us when nobody in town has a hangnail that needs his attention. Didn't he tell you who he was?"

"Who?"

"The man you followed out here. Doc Barkley."

Morris's eyes drifted to where the buckboard had vanished from view within the walls. "He's a doctor?"

"That's what they claim. Can be a real old bastard when he wants to. As a medical man, it gives you something to look forward to in your old age, doesn't it?"

"He didn't look like a doctor to me," Morris said somewhat stiffly. "If anything, I took him for a local merchant."

"Some folks around here might agree with that assessment," Kincaid offered with a chuckle, "but out here you make do with the best you can. Didn't he talk to you on the way out from town?"

"No, sir. I met him on the road, and asked him the direction

25

to your outpost. He told me to follow him, and when I tried to introduce myself in a civil manner, he said something like, 'If I wanted to talk, young fella, I would have been a barber,' then drove away.''

"Might have missed his calling at that," Kincaid said, dismissing the topic and turning to Sergeant Cohen. "All right, Sergeant, let's get to it. Guidon and flags lowered, have Reb blow taps. We'll want the honor guard to fire a volley over the grave, the whole thing. Jenkins was the last of his kind that we know of, and the captain wants him to go out with full ceremony."

"Yes, sir. How about the flag over the coffin, Lieutenant?"

"Save it. We'll be needing it again, I'm sure."

When the last strains of the plaintive bugle call had melted into the balmy air of the spring-like afternoon and the company had been dismissed, Kincaid and the new second lieutenant led their mounts toward the compound. Morris withdrew the packet of papers from his pocket and passed them across to Kincaid, saying, "Here are my orders, sir. If you would be so kind as to have someone show me to the surgery—" He caught the bemused expression on Kincaid's face, and said, "Certainly some accommodation has been set aside for care of the sick and wounded."

"Yes, it has. Your quarters, to be specific. We're a little cramped for space, and for the time being at least, your office, your quarters, and your surgery will be one and the same."

"If you'll pardon my saying so, Lieutenant, that's a bit primitive, isn't it?"

"There are few things you'll find out here that aren't primitive, and one learns damned quick to improvise and make do the best one can, and that goes for all professions, yours as well as mine. We'll do what we can to get you set up properly, of course, but don't expect a hell of a lot."

"I'll have to admit, Lieutenant," Morris said with a sideways glance as they neared the BOQ, "there isn't much that could surprise me more than what I've seen already."

"Sure, there is," Kincaid replied, looping his reins around a rail in front of the BOQ and stepping onto the walkway. "For starters, there's a woman dying in your quarters right now."

"What? A woman?"

"You heard me. Young, pretty, damned near dead, and a certain candidate for the hangman's noose. Come on, Doc

Barkley might be able to use your help."

Morris hesitated on the planking in front of the doorway. "The hangman's noose, sir? I'm afraid I don't understand."

"That's the accepted punishment for cattle stealing out here, Lieutenant. The way the local law sees it, a pretty neck breaks just as legally at the end of a rope as an ugly one. Oh, by the way," Kincaid said, pausing with his hand on the latch, "she's also being held on a murder charge. Same rope, same punishment."

The look on Morris's face was one of stunned disbelief as they stepped into the smallish room, barren of furniture with the exception of a cot against one wall, and a table upon which lay an exceptionally pretty young lady. With Flora Conway and Maggie Cohen standing close by, Doc Barkley hovered over the patient. Wearing the same duster he had worn upon arrival, and with the familiar cigar clenched in his teeth, he probed the shoulder wound with pudgy fingers while his ample stomach rested comfortably on the edge of the table. It was obvious that his nails hadn't been cleaned prior to the examination, and a bead of sweat had formed on his bulbous nose and appeared about to drip into the wound.

Kincaid started to make the introductions, then nodded his assent as Flora held a finger to her lips. He stepped forward and tapped the physician lightly on a rounded, sloping shoulder.

"Barkley," he began in a low tone, "I have a man here with me who might be able to assist you with whatever needs to be done. He is a medical man, trained at the University of Pennsylvania, and a practicing physician."

Barkley looked up with a scowl and craned his neck to peer over his shoulder. "Him?"

"Yes. Dr. Barkley, meet Dr. Morris."

"Pleased to meet you, Doctor," Morris offered in a less-than-confident tone.

Barkley grunted and turned back to his work. "Don't need any help from a schoolboy. Besides, she won't live out the day. I'll take the bullet out, but gangrene has already set in. The poison won't be long in coming."

"Excuse me, Lieutenant," Morris said, stepping forward for a closer look at the purplish-black hole, swollen now and caked with blood. "Mind if I have a look, Doctor?"

Barkley shifted grudgingly to one side, but only slightly as he glanced up at Flora. "I'll need my scalpel and that pair of tweezers out of my bag, Mrs. Conway."

Flora moved toward the bag, then stopped with Morris's sharply spoken words. "No, ma'am. Wait one minute, please." He leaned closer to the wound and examined it without touching his hand to the flesh. There was a look of transformation about him, the look of a man who had suddenly stepped from an alien existence and into his own world—a world in which he was entirely professional and completely in charge.

"Do you wish to kill her, Doctor?" he asked softly, glancing up from his brief inspection.

"What?" Barkley asked, his tone both defensive and demanding.

"I said, do you wish to kill her?"

"If I wanted to see her dead, I sure as hell wouldn't have rode all the way out here, young fella." His hot gaze went to Flora once more. "The scalpel, if you please, Mrs. Conway."

"No!" Morris said firmly. "Not just now. This wound must be sterilized, as well as your hands and surgical equipment. There is infection now, and it will certainly spread if not properly contained. You mentioned gangrene, but I see no sign of it as yet. The wound is severely discolored from lack of oxygen, which will certainly lead to gangrene if it is not opened and allowed to cleanse itself and gain oxygen through bleeding."

Barkley stepped back while snatching up a soiled cloth, and angrily wiped the blood from his hands before tossing the rag to one side. Jerking the cigar from his mouth, he jabbed it toward Morris while saying, "Just who the hell do you think you are, young fella? I'll tell you who you are—a damned young whippersnapper with the ink still wet on his medical degree. If I don't get that bullet out of there damned quick, she's good as gone. And let me tell you one more thing—I know gangrene when I see it, and that's what I'm lookin' at right here!"

While it was obvious that Barkley was becoming personally agitated, it was equally clear that Morris was professionally excited and becoming more impassioned with each word, although outwardly attempting to control his emotions.

"What you are looking at, sir, is a woman who is suffering from a high fever resulting from a combination of the severity of her wounds and the attendant stress upon her system in tandem with a manifest spread of germs through lack of proper disinfection. Antisepsis, prior to and during surgery to remove

28

the bullet is her only hope of survival."

"Anti . . . what?"

"Antisepsis, sir."

"What the hell is that?" Barkley asked.

"Have you read of the findings of Semmelweis?" Morris continued with a deeply sincere, almost passionate reverence for the subject.

"No. 'Round here there's damned little time for reading."

"Then perhaps Joseph Lister? Louis Pasteur? It's in all the latest medical journals."

A quarter-inch ash fell on Barkley's vest, and he brushed it away with a flick of his hand. "I told you, dammit, I don't read! I do what has to be done, *when* it has to be done! And if you're talking about some of this modern tomfoolery, I'd just as lief trust my own personal judgment over witchcraft." His eyes narrowed and his chest swelled nearly to bursting. "Now, young man, either that bullet comes out by my hand, here and now, or I go with a clear conscience and leave the fate of that young woman there to your devices. Which will it be?"

There was complete silence until Kincaid said quietly, "Can't understand a thing you've said so far, Lieutenant, but it sounds like you know what you're talking about. Don't back away now if you're sure you're right."

Kincaid's words seemed to give the young doctor the confidence he needed, and he quickly turned again to Barkley. "Doctor, I am not trying to undermine your medical integrity, or attempting to show off a superior grasp of the science. But there is irrefutable evidence proving that antisepsis, which is the process of sterilizing the wound, surgical equipment, dressings, and"—he couldn't avoid a glance at Barkley's blood-encrusted hands—"even the hands of the surgeons that might come in contact with the area upon which the operation is to be performed, is vital to the hope of preventing life-threatening infection. The important word is *preventing,* doctor, rather than post-operative *treatment*. That is what antisepsis is all about."

Whether from conscious embarrassment or merely from habit, Barkley clasped his thick hands behind his back and puffed several times on his cigar. "Well, ain't this somethin'?" he asked derisively. "I've delivered more young'uns, set more bones, dug out more bullets, and sawed off more arms than you've got hairs in your beard, and you come in here tellin' me about some newfangled notion about how to do doctor work. Let me tell you, young fella, there's many a man settin' a saddle right now that wouldn't be if it hadn't been for my doctorin' know-how."

"I'm sure there are," Morris said coolly.

Barkley worked the cigar back and forth in his mouth for long moments before saying, "God takes 'em when he wants 'em, son. Neither you nor I have anything to say about that." Then he smiled in cruel triumph. "What say you operate on that little gal over there, and I'll just stand here and wait till you need me?" Then he smiled in cruel triumph. "That is, unless she dies first, of course."

Without hesitation, Morris unbuttoned his tunic, draped it over a chair, and began rolling up his sleeves. "That's fine with me, Doctor, and you're welcome to stay in the hope that you might observe something that could be beneficial to your patients in the future. But before I begin, there's one thing I must insist upon."

"What's that?" Barkley asked, raising an eyebrow quizically.

"The cigar has to go."

"What?"

"The cigar has to go. Until I leave here, there will be no further smoking in this surgery, and especially when an operation is in progress."

"Well...I...you...you're absolutely mad!" Barkley spluttered. "Mad! Stark raving mad!" the old doctor screamed, lunging forward to snatch up his satchel and jerk his hat from the rack before lurching toward the door. He plopped his hat on his head and turned as he stepped onto the boardwalk. "If that girl dies," he said, jabbing the cigar through the air between clenched thumb and forefinger once more, "I'm going to hold you personally responsible! And that goes for you too, Lieutenant Kincaid!" he snarled as the door slammed behind him.

Morris looked at Kincaid in the heavy silence. "Are you with me, sir?" he asked as he looked unblinkingly at the executive officer.

"One hundred percent, Lieutenant. Tell us what you need and how we can help. The rest of it is up to you."

"Good. Please get my medical bag from behind my saddle and bring it in here, sir. Then—"

"Forget the 'sir' for now, Lieutenant," Kincaid interjected.

"This is no time for formalities."

"Excellent. When you get the bag back, find a bottle of carbolic acid and open it for one of the ladies. Then find a textbook in one of my saddlebags entitled *Surgical Procedures for the Chest and Upper Torso.* Turn it to chapter twelve and be prepared to read the answer to any question I might ask."

Next he turned to Flora and Maggie. "Ladies, I'll need some exceptionally hot water, some clean rags, and several folds of clean cheesecloth or gauze to place over the woman's mouth and nose. When the lieutenant returns with the carbolic acid, mix one part acid to thirty parts water in one basin, and three parts to thirty in the other. In the first one, I'll sterilize my surgical equipment, which you'll find in the bag, and the other will be used to cleanse the wound. I'll disinfect my hands in the first basin after the equipment has been thoroughly cleansed."

Morris was talking rapidly and confidently. His eyes constantly went to the wound and the patient's face as he laid out his equipment for sterilization, and he continued to instruct in a calm, authoritative voice:

"We will be utilizing a new form of anesthesia called ether, and I will need one of you to be constantly prepared to add the drops to the cloth over the patient's nose when asked, but only when requested. The other one will assist in the operation by passing to me whichever device I ask for, and be prepared for the possibility of physical contact with the wound or incision. You will both disinfect your hands as well, and avoid breathing on the exposed flesh at all times. No one is to enter or leave until the operation is concluded."

There was such an aura of total command about the young doctor that his three assistants complied with his clearly stated requests without hesitation or doubt. After the antisepsis procedure had been completed, Maggie stood over the patient, carefully applying drops of ether to the cloth, and Flora stood by Morris's side while Kincaid stood to the rear with the medical book opened to the requested chapter.

When Morris asked for the scalpel, Flora handed it across and watched as the razor-sharp blade was poised over tender flesh and drawn down in a testing arc; then it kissed white skin, and fresh blood seeped forth. Both Maggie and Flora closed their eyes and glanced away. Without looking up, Morris sensed their repulsion.

"Don't feel ashamed and don't be alarmed by your reaction. I felt the same way, and I'll tell you now, this is the first time I've seen it myself on a live human being. I need your help and so does she. Please dab that blood away with one of the cloths soaked in carbolic, and I think we should have another drop of ether."

Both women complied while Morris spoke over his shoulder. "Look up the *latissimus dorsi* muscle, Lieutenant. I'll need to know what tissue it overlaps, because the bullet has obviously penetrated that area. From the angle of entry, I believe it might be lodged beneath the clavicle, so find the *sternocleidomastoid* muscle as well, and mark the place with one finger. We'll need that section later. I suspect there might be some damage to the *pectoralis major* also, but we'll be able to tell better when we get in more deeply."

Nearly twenty minutes passed, with Kincaid reading from the textbook when asked to, Flora alternately wiping sweat from the doctor's brow and passing him the requested surgical devices, and Maggie carefully dampening the cloth with ether upon a nod from Morris. Kincaid couldn't help but marvel at the studied efficiency of the same man whom he had held in slight contempt only an hour before, and he wondered briefly at the narrow capacity of one human's ability to judge another merely upon a first impression.

Finally the doctor made a last, testing probe with the forceps, hesitated momentarily, and then straightened with the first smile he had offered since the operation had begun. Held in the pincers grip of the slim instrument was a flattened piece of lead resembling a tiny mushroom.

"There it is," he said, holding the bullet up to the light for examination. "It appears to be intact, with no splintering or fragmentation." He extended the slug for Kincaid to see. "What do you think, Lieutenant? You know more about these things than I do."

"I think that's all of it. They're made of pretty soft lead, and its not very often that any breaks off."

"Good. All we have to do now is throughly disinfect the wound, close the incision, and then bandage." He paused and there seemed to be a twinkle in his eyes as he concluded, "On that point, your Dr. Barkley is entirely correct. The rest of it is up to God."

After the wound had been closed and bandaged, Morris

washed his hands a final time and glanced up at Flora, then across to Maggie. "Thank you for your help. I couldn't have done it without you. And you too, Lieutenant. Now, allow me to formally introduce myself—I'm Dr. Frederick Morris."

Matt closed the medical book and stepped forward. "The lady across from you is Mrs. Conway, Doctor, the wife of our commanding officer whom you met earlier."

A blush crept into Morris's cheeks, and he immediately became subservient in his manner. "I'm sorry, Mrs. Conway. Here I am, ordering the captain's lady about without so much as a by-your-leave, and within the first hour of my first assignment."

"The other lady is Mrs. Cohen," Matt went on, "the wife of our first sergeant. You haven't met him yet, but I can assure you that once you do, you won't soon forget him."

Morris replied, "I can assure *you,* Lieutenant, that I won't soon forget *Mrs.* Cohen, and her steady hand with the ether bottle."

"Posh," Maggie said with a dimpled smile. "If it was me lying on that table, I'd be wanting you bossing folks like us around myself."

"Maggie's absolutely correct, Doctor," Flora offered, laying a hand tenderly on the young lieutenant's arm. "You did exactly what you had to do, and God bless you for that. Will she be all right?"

"I think so," Morris replied, wiping his fingers one final time before laying the cloth aside. "It'll take some time for her to come out of the ether, and there might be some nausea, but other than that, she should be as good as new with proper bed rest and care. She's a lucky woman, and quite strong, I might add. Even at that, I doubt she could have survived another day."

Flora glanced at Kincaid and then dabbed a cool cloth on the young woman's forehead. "Let's hope she survives many more days to come, Doctor. I suspect her travail is not over with the removal of a bullet. She's really quite beautiful, don't you think?"

Morris looked down at his patient, and a different expression filled his eyes, as though he were seeing her for the first time. There was a tender gentleness about his face as he watched her in momentary silence.

33

"Yes, she certainly is," he said softly in a tone that might indicate that the two of them were alone in the room. "Very beautiful. Strange, but I hadn't noticed before."

three ——————————————

"If she's alive, I want her back! Do you understand that? I want her back, no matter what it takes, and I don't give one good goddamn in hell who has to die in the process!!!"

The speaker, a huge bearded man, ranged back and forth across the earthen floor of a small cabin snuggled against the leeward side of a rolling prairie knoll. He banged a massive fist against the log wall as he turned for another angry surge across the room. A long bowie knife was strapped to one side of his gunbelt, while a Colt .44 hung from the other. His red flannel shirt sagged open, exposing a barrel chest matted with thick black hair. One corner of his mouth was twisted in a permanent sneer, the result of a knife fight years ago, and his dark eyes glittered with hatred as he spun in the center of the room to face his three companions.

"Is that perfectly clear to you stupid assholes?"

The three, two white men and a half-breed, nodded in silence as they watched their leader warily. The eldest of the three was rather small of stature and might well have passed as a cowhand down on his luck. The second was young, tall, and slender, and wore moderately expensive clothing, while the third was scraggly-haired and wore a headband and dirty buckskin garments. He obviously favored his Sioux mother more than he did his Caucasian father.

The big man's eyes held on the half-breed and he jabbed a dirty forefinger toward the man's chest. "You, Charlie One-Jump, you said you saw the whole damned thing. I want to hear it, top to bottom, and don't leave one goddamn word out! You other two had better listen good," he snarled, jerking the cork from a whiskey bottle with his teeth and pouring generously into a dented tin cup. "'Cause if he's lyin' like the Indian in him wants to, your asses'll all be hung out to dry. Let's hear it, Charlie."

The man called Charlie One-Jump smiled in a sick, almost demented way, as was his nature, and watched his leader swill the whiskey down, wipe his mouth angrily with the back of a filthy sleeve, then pour again.

"You gonna share some of that with us, Slate?" the breed asked, his voice surprisingly indicating no fear.

"Hell, no! You don't deserve it. Now get on with the tellin'!"

The breed merely shrugged and continued to smile. "Sure, Slate, whatever you want. Me, Reeves, and Shorty there took the first bunch of government beef on down to the lower brakes, just like you told us to do, and we waited there for Harmon and his bunch to show up like you said. It started to rain pretty hard, and after a while I went back to find them, leavin' Reeves and Shorty with the herd. When I first saw them from a distance, Harmon was on the far side of his herd, talkin' to a bunch of bluelegs. Seein' that, I knew their fat was in the fire so I kinda hid back out of sight and watched. Pretty soon, Harmon and two soldiers rode toward the herd..."

"Where was Lee Ellen?" Jake Slater snapped.

"Toward the front of the herd, with Bixby."

"Go on."

"I was too far away to see exactly what was goin' on, but I heard a shot, saw one soldier take a bullet, then Harmon and the others rode like hell for a place we call Alder's Ravine. It was the worst place they could have gone, 'cause there ain't no way out the back.

"Don't think he'd of had much luck, Slate. Them bluelegs was comin' toward the herd to check the brands. Anyway, all the army had to do was seal off the ravine and wait for 'em to come out once the creek filled with water, which they did, right enough. Harmon came out first, then Bixby, then Coalie. Lee Ellen was the last. All four of 'em were shot off their horses, but I thought for a minute your woman might get away. Didn't happen, though, and she was picked off just before she got out of range. The soldier boys packed her up, along with their dead one, an took her with them." The breed searched his mind and then shrugged. "That's it. That's all there is to tell. Now how 'bout a drink?"

"Not so fast," Slater snapped, jerking the bottle back out of the breed's grasp. "Did you check to make sure the others were dead? We don't need nobody gettin' a sudden urge for honesty right about now."

"I did. They were all dead. I went back and got Reeves and Shorty and we rounded up the other herd and moved 'em down to the brakes with the rest. Rain wiped out our tracks, and nobody'll find 'em unless they stumble on to 'em. Now, I'm needin' a drink after all that talkin'. How 'bout it?"

Grudgingly, Slater passed the bottle across, and all three men drank deeply when their turns came. With one boot propped on a chair, Slater fingered his beard and stared at the floor while he spoke in a studied tone, as though sorting out the pieces to a puzzle all his own.

"If they took Lee Ellen with them, that means she must be alive, or at least she was when they picked her up. She's got too much fear in her to talk out of turn, 'cause she knows I'll find her and bring her back, just like I done afore. She knows it ain't healthy for her to get me grizzly mad. Never hit her or beat her or nothin' like that—she's too purty to be put to the knuckles. But I sure do know the kind of punishment she understands, and the kind she ain't likely to forget. Done it to her every time she's run away, and I'll by damn—"

Slater's head jerked up with a start and he glared at his companions. "You boys didn't hear nothin' what I said, did ya?"

The three men glanced self-consciously at each other and shook their heads. "Didn't hear a word, Slate," the one called

Reeves said cautiously. "My mind was on the whiskey, and I thought you was just talkin' to yourself."

"I was, and I don't like nobody listenin' in." Slater rose to his full height, crossed the room in three strides, and jerked the bottle from Shorty's hand. "You fellers has had enough. You've got work to do. Shorty, I want you to go into town and see if anybody has asked to have the doctor fetched out to the post. You should make it back here afore nightfall. If they have"—his gaze shifted to the tall, moderately handsome younger man—"you head on in to the post afore dawn tomorrow morning. Tell 'em you got some kin sick and need the doctor's advice. Tell 'em anything, but make sure you get in to where Lee Ellen is. Find out if she's dead or alive. If she's dead, we can forget her." Now Slater gazed deeply into the bottle and swirled the whiskey in his hand. "If she's alive, I want her back. She's mine, and ain't nobody ever gonna take her away from me. Now get crackin', Shorty. Bring back a couple more jugs when ya come."

As Shorty headed for the door, Slater looked again at the half-breed. "Dobler should be here in a few days to take that stock off our hands and pay us for our honest labor. How long do you think it'll take workin' like this to get Kills Many Bear and Beaver Claw at each other's throats?"

"Not long, Slate. They are both powerful chiefs and that makes them rivals. Beaver Claw is a medicine chief and Kills Many Bear is a war chief, like I told you before. Kills Many Bear signed the treaty with the white men, and he believes the government will supply the beef they have promised to the Sioux. Beaver Claw doesn't think so, and if he can prove Kills Many Bear is wrong, that will show he has stronger medicine, and the two of them will have to fight for leadership of the tribe. When that happens, the army will have a medicine war on their hands, and when the Sioux turn their hatred on each other, blood will flow like water in the streams." Charlie One-Jump smiled in cold, distant satisfaction. "Beaver Claw doesn't know it, but we're giving him all the help he needs to prove that he has the stronger medicine. A few more head that don't get delivered should be about enough to do it."

Slater unconsciously reached up and touched the scar across the corner of his mouth. "You told us that a medicine war was the worst kind, and if we can get that stirred up, both the Sioux and the damned army'll be too damned busy chasin' each other to come lookin' for us. Ain't that right?"

"That's right, and we're close to one now."

"Good, 'cause if we have to go huntin' on the reservation for that money, we'll need a damned good cover. When we find it, we'll make the split and go our separate ways." Slater gazed at the open doorway and he said just above a graveled whisper, "Fifty thousand dollars might just make Lee Ellen take a little better shine to me than she does now. But, as things stand, I need her for a helluva lot more'n she needs me. Damn old Dugan for givin' her his half of the map after we went to prison. Now she's the only one who can lead us back to the spot where her pappy hid that cash after we split with that posse on our trail."

Matt Kincaid looked at the packet of orders one final time, then folded them and rose to leave his quarters. Even though they had been given to him two days before, upon Morris's arrival, it was the first time he had had a chance to study them closely. At first glance it had appeared that the young medical man had arrived at his assigned post, but now, upon further scrutiny, he was certain that some clerk back at headquarters had made a mistake in drawing up the orders. It was midafternoon when he pulled on his hat, closed the door behind him, and hurried across the parade.

"Lieutenant Kincaid?"

Matt slowed near the flagpole and turned toward the main gate. "Yes, Corporal?"

"There's a man here who wants to see the officer in charge, sir! He says it's urgent."

Anxious to pass his findings about Lieutenant Morris's billeting error to the captain, Kincaid hesitated momentarily, then turned toward the sentry. "Show him in, Corporal. I'll see what he wants."

As Matt approached the wall, he saw the gates open and watched a tall, slender man mounted on a sorrel horse nod politely to the guard while he urged his mount inside. They met at the midpoint between the flagpole and the gate and Kincaid looked up, shielding his eyes from the brilliant sun.

"My name is Lieutenant Kincaid. Can I help you?"

The handsome but strangely hardened rider smiled with disarming cordiality. "I'm Dennis Harper, Lieutenant. Pleased to make your acquaintance and thank you for seeing me," he said, turning in his saddle and glancing casually around the post. Apparently seeing nothing to hold his interest, he turned back to Kincaid. "I've got a problem, Lieutenant. I mean, my brother has. I started in to town to find a doctor, but somebody told me he had come out here. My brother's sick, bad sick."

"I'm sorry to hear that, Mr. Harper, but the doctor has come and gone. He should have been back to town by now. Where's your brother?"

"We made camp about five, maybe seven miles from here. He ain't going to die or nothin' like that, I don't think, but he's in real bad pain. Seems to be his stomach. I was hoping to get some laudanum or something to ease the pain so we could make it to town and get him treated proper."

"Where are you and your brother heading?"

"Out West, but I don't know rightly for sure. Anywhere we can find work, I guess," the young man added with a weak grin.

"Shouldn't be too hard for you to find a decent job," Matt replied, noticing the stock saddle, chaps, and coiled rope. "Should be plenty of cattle work."

"That's kinda what we're lookin' for, but a job right now isn't the most important thing to my mind. God, I hate to leave my brother in that kind of pain long enough to ride clean back to town, find that damned doctor, and get back to him again. Guess I ain't got much choice, though, unless you've got some laudanum for your soldier boys around here that I could get. Be willin' to pay for it, and a good price to boot."

Kincaid shook his head and smiled. "We're not in the business of selling medicine, Mr. Harper, but I might be able to help you. We've got a doctor of our own here now, at least temporarily, and I'm sure he'll be able to help you. He's got a severely wounded patient on his hands at present, and wouldn't be able to leave to tend to your brother, but he might be able to spare some laudanum."

The young man's eyes seemed to brighten at the mention of a severely wounded patient, but his expression remained one of concern and understanding. "I wouldn't ask that of him, no sir. If he's got somebody hurt real bad, I sure wouldn't expect him to leave just to take care of a bellyache. How bad is the poor feller hurt?"

"Gunshot wound through the shoulder. Bad, but not fatal. The doctor thinks she'll live and be up and around in a week or so." Kincaid didn't notice the sly grin on the man's face at the mention of the patient's sex because he had turned away to point out the makeshift dispensary. "You should be able to find the doctor with her now, over there. His name is Dr. Morris, and he doesn't want his patient disturbed, so knock gently on the door, then talk with him outside. I would show you to him personally, but I've got some important matters to discuss with the post commander."

"Not at all," the man said with a wide, affable grin. "You tend to your army business and don't worry about me. I can find that doctor just fine by myself. Mind if I water my horse before I leave?"

"Help yourself. Good day, Mr. Harper. I hope the doctor can help you and that your brother is back on his feet before too long."

"He will be, Lieutenant. I can assure you, he will be. It's been a pleasure meetin' you, and you've been more of a help than you could possibly know. Much obliged."

"Glad I could help," Kincaid replied, turning away while pulling the packet of papers from his pocket once more and studying them as he moved toward the orderly room.

There was a cold, satisfied expression on the lean rider's face as he waited until Kincaid had disappeared inside before dismounting and leading his horse to a water trough, while never taking his eyes from the closed door of the surgery.

"Good afternoon, Ben," Kincaid said as he stepped into the orderly room. "Hard at it I see."

Ben Cohen looked up from the requisition forms strewn across his desktop. "Hello, sir. Quartermaster doesn't seem to have ever heard of that old biblical line about, 'ask and ye shall receive.'" He waved a hand disgustedly toward the forms. "Rejected. Every damned one of 'em rejected."

Kincaid laughed as he moved toward the door to the captain's office. "There's something else about, 'if at first you don't succeed, try, try again.' Looks like that's our lot in life. The captain in?"

"Yes, sir. Just knock and let yourself in."

"Thanks," Kincaid said, then paused with knuckles raised. "Has Maggie been over to see the patient yet today? I haven't made it down there yet myself."

"Yes, she has. Says the woman's conscious, but if she can speak, she hasn't so far. The doc seems to think she's in some

41

kind of mental state, shocked into silence by what's happening to her now or what happened somewhere in her past. I guess he's going to try to get her to open up a little this afternoon."

"I hope he can. We've got a few questions to ask her ourselves, but we'd prefer to wait until she gets a little more strength back. Let me know if there's any change."

"I'll do that, sir."

"Thanks, Ben," Kincaid replied, rapping twice and then opening the captain's door a crack. "Got a minute, sir?"

"Sure, Matt. Come on in. What have you got?"

Kincaid closed the door while the captain leaned back in his chair and folded his fingers across his stomach. Matt snapped the creases from the papers as he approached the desk to spread them out before Conway.

"You were right, sir. We've got a doctor, but he doesn't belong to us," Kincaid said, moving around the desk and trailing his finger down the first page. "Here, on page one, Morris is clearly assigned to Post Number Nine—not *Out*post Number Nine—on the billeting order. But then, see here, on the third and fourth pages," he continued flipping the standard forms, "Post Number Ninety appears twice, and the zero has been scratched out both times, but it's still legible."

"I see," Conway replied, studying the forms. "Apparently some clerk made a mistake, and with Morris still pissing civilian water, as it were, he didn't have enough sense to realize that a mistake had been made. Where the hell is Post Number Ninety, anyway?"

Kincaid turned to the map tacked against the wall behind the captain's desk, studied the legend, and then located the area. "Post Number Ninety is Fort McDowell, Arizona, sir. He only missed his proper duty assignment by a thousand miles or so. Not bad," Kincaid added with a grin, "for the first time out."

Conway sighed and leaned back once more. "Well, perhaps it was providential. That woman down there in the BOQ wouldn't be alive now if he hadn't wandered into the wrong post, if what you and Flora tell me is correct, as I'm sure it is."

"Absolutely correct, Captain. Even though he seems kind of shy and awkward about other things, the man is a geniune marvel when it comes to medicine. You would've had to see it to believe the way he took charge before and during the

42

operation. He's a totally different person when a human life is in danger."

"It's a shame we can't keep him. How long do you think it'll take to get this mess straightened out?"

"Anywhere from a month to a year, Captain. As you know, it's damned near impossible to get headquarters to admit they've made a mistake, then when and if they do, it takes an eternity for them to correct it. But one thing I know for sure, he has to stay here until this thing is straightened out through proper channels."

"Yes, and I'll be glad to have him as long as he is legitimately ours," Conway replied, rising and moving to the window. "Did you have any luck rounding up the cattle that were lost when Olsen jumped those rustlers?"

"No, sir. They were gone, as well as any tracks, which were washed out by the rain. Maybe Windy could have picked up something, but I couldn't find a damned thing."

"When is he due back?"

"Tomorrow or the next day. He said he was going to stop by and talk with old Roy Stearns, the agent over at the Sioux reservation. He thinks there might be some bad blood building between Kills Many Bear and Beaver Claw. If those two go at it, it could be real trouble."

"Yes, I'm sure. When he gets back, fill him in on what's been happening. Has the doctor gotten anything out of the woman yet? For some reason, I'd like to have her dealt with more as a patient than a prisoner for the time being, but we've got to stop the rustling and get some cattle to those Sioux before they say to hell with the treaty. If she's got anything to say, we'd better get it out of her damned quick."

"Ben told me that Morris was going to try to talk to her this afternoon, sir. I'll stop by there later on, and, if he's had any luck, maybe she'll talk to me."

"Good, Matt. Notify headquarters about Lieutenant Morris's being here, and wait for them to make the next move, all right?"

"Fine, sir." Matt said, rising and moving toward the door. "I'll send a wire right now."

At the precise moment Kincaid left the orderly room and crossed to the telegraph shack, Morris was leaning on the side of the bed and looking down at the woman whose life he had saved. The first signs of pink vitality had returned to her cheeks. Even though no words had been exchanged, doctor and patient

43

had been together continuously for forty-eight hours, and Morris, as he watched over her late in the night, had developed a strong attachment to the woman.

Once, when he had been checking her pulse, she had gripped his hand and clung to it until the nightmare racing through her mind passed and she sank again into a troubled sleep. Morris had refrained from asking any questions during her moments of semiconsciousness, but now, as she stared blankly at the ceiling, he leaned toward her and offered a smile.

"How are you feeling?" he asked gently.

No response, not even a flicker of the eyes.

"My name is Dr. Frederick Morris." he continued with gentle but professional firmness, "and I am the physician who treated your wound. You've been a sick young lady for a long time now—nearly two and a half days—but you're making remarkable progress."

A blink, nothing more.

"Who are you? I'd like to know your name."

There was a hesitation, then a slight, barely perceptible negative shake of her head.

Morris's heart skipped a beat. At last some response, however remote. "Does your family live near here?"

Her mouth formed a silent "no" and a film of moisture touched her lashes when she blinked again. Morris hesitated, studying his mind, searching for questions that would compel her to speak but not unduly frighten her.

"Are you feeling any pain?"

Again, a negative shake of the head.

"That's good. It means that the swelling has stopped and the pressure is less against your wound. If you do feel extreme pain, however, I can give you something for that." Once more, Morris smiled warmly. "Won't you tell me your name? We're going to be together for quite a while yet, and it would be much more convenient if we could address each other properly."

She hesitated, obviously making a decision, and then her head turned on the pillow. Her silky auburn hair contrasted sharply with the white linen. Her eyes held upon him, and he perceived in their depths the simultaneous emotions of animal fear and the need to trust, to reach out and communicate with another human being.

"Don't be afraid of me," Morris said gently, taking her hand in his and sensing the immediate instinct to withdraw, followed by a relaxation of tensed muscles. "I am your friend, or I would like to be, and I am also your doctor. Nothing you say to me will go beyond this room. After all, I saved your life once, and I wouldn't like to see it jeopardized a second time."

Her answer came weakly, but after such a long silence it startled Morris like a gunshot.

"Why?"

"Why, what?"

"Why did you save my life?"

The simple question stunned him. "Why? Because that's what I was trained to do, and I took an oath more sacred to me than any other thing I know."

"An oath?" she asked, her eyes searching his face.

"Yes, an oath. Part of it says, 'Into whatever houses I enter, I will go into them for the benefit of the sick.' Then it goes on to say: 'Whatever in connection with my professional practice, or not in connection with it, I see or hear, in the life of men, which ought not to be spoken of abroad, I will not divulge as reckoning that all such should be kept secret.'" He smiled. "So, for the same reason that I won't divulge anything you might say to me, I saved your life, even though I don't know you."

She closed her eyes tightly and turned her head away. "Then you are wrong to do what you have done."

"Wrong? How was I wrong?"

"Because you had no right to save my life, no matter what your stupid oath may cause you to believe. I don't want to live. I want to die. I should have had that one right, if no other."

"But why? Why would you want to die?" Morris asked, genuinely appalled. "You are a beautiful . . ." He caught himself and blushed immediately. "I'm sorry. I shouldn't have said that."

Her head turned toward him and there was a hint of a smile at the corners of her mouth. "Why? Why shouldn't you have said that, if you really mean it? Is it another part of your stupid oath?"

"Well, I guess it could be construed to mean that in some ways, but that's not the reason I felt I shouldn't have said what I did. Mainly, it's because I don't know you and that, as your doctor, I shouldn't take advantage of a patient-physician relationship."

A hint of mischievous joy filled her face and she said quickly, "My name is Lee Ellen Dugan, and you are Dr. Frederick Morris. Now, we know each other. Do you still think I'm beautiful?"

"Yes. Very much so."

"No one ever told me that before, except my father"—her eyelids fluttered and she looked down at the comforter across her chest—"and I never saw very much of him. He was gone most of the time when I was young, and I was raised by my aunt until she passed away."

"What does your father do? For a living, I mean."

"He was a bank robber. The last time I saw him was in prison, and that was ten years ago."

Morris could scarcely believe the passionless manner in which Lee Ellen was revealing her past to him. "Is he still alive?" he asked.

"I don't know. I've been told that he is, but I don't know for sure."

"I'm sorry, Lee Ellen. I really am."

She pressed her lips together and looked at Morris with a tight smile. "Don't be. My past and my problems are mine alone to live with." Again she looked away. "Or die with, if I have my way."

"Come on now, Lee Ellen," Morris said with artificial brightness as he squeezed her hand. "As your doctor and your friend, I don't even want to hear that kind of talk."

"I've been to prison to see my father, Doctor, and I couldn't stand to be sent there myself. I know what they have in mind for me, what with the stolen cattle and all, and I know what the outcome will be. I would rather die than be sent to prison, or face again the existence that I knew before I was shot. That's why I wish you would not have saved my life. It would have been much simpler that way."

Morris held his breath, calculating, trying to make the right decision. Then he asked, "Did you help steal those cattle?"

"No," Lee Ellen answered simply.

"But you know who did?"

"Yes."

"Then it's simple," Morris said, unconsciously edging forward on his chair. "You merely tell the law who did it."

Lee Ellen looked at him like a mother might at an innocent child. "You're sweet, Dr. Morris, but you're also much too naive for life out here. No one would believe me, even if I did testify against Sla—" She caught herself. "Even if I did testify.

46

And besides, he or one of his men would kill me if I did anyway, so what's the difference?"

"That's impossible! Beyond belief! Certainly there is some justice even in this barbaric place!"

"Yes, there is. It's called frontier justice. Let the big dog eat, that sort of thing. Unfortunately, I'm not a big dog, and with my father's reputation hanging over my head I could not possibly hope to have a jury decide a case in my favor." Now her hand squeezed his, almost tenderly. "But thank you anyway. You are truly the first person who has cared enough even to concern himself since my aunt died."

Morris glanced around the room and held his palms up in helpless frustration. "Surely there's some way. Tell me who the guilty ones are, and I'll talk to Lieutenant Kincaid. I hardly know him, but I am an excellent judge of character. He would help, I'm sure he would."

"There's nothing he can do!"

"At least we can try! We've got to try!"

"Do you think," she asked, looking again at Morris with a hint of hope in her eyes, "do you really think he might believe me? Give me a chance to prove my innocence?"

"Yes. Yes, I do. But you'll have to trust us, and the first sign of that trust is to tell us who the guilty ones are. Would you do that?"

"I . . . I don't know. If he ever takes me again, I . . . I just don't know."

"Please, Lee Ellen. It's the only way. Trust me, and if you decide later that you don't want to go through with it, I give you my solemn promise that the name will never pass my lips. Please, Lee Ellen. The only way I can help you is if you help yourself. He took her face in his hands and turned it toward him. "You said a name in your delirium several times, and I'm going to ask you if he is the man. If he is, you just nod, you don't have to say anything. All right?"

Again the tears touched the corners of her eyes, and she bit at her trembling lip while nodding with the tiniest of movements.

"Good. Very good. Now listen to me closely, because you never said his name very clearly in your sleep. Is it—Slater?"

Lee Ellen's eyes widened and she looked at Morris in frozen shock. She opened her mouth to speak while starting to move her head, then there came a sharp rapping at the door.

Her head jerked toward the alien sound like that of a startled animal, and her body jerked convusively beneath the covers."

"Damn," Morris muttered, then patted her hand reassuringly. "Now don't be frightened. It's probably just someone with a message for me. Relax a moment, I'll see who it is, then I'll come back and we'll take up where we left off. All right?"

Lee Ellen nodded, but her eyes were locked on the door.

"That's fine, I won't be but a moment," Morris said, rising and crossing the room. He opened the door just wide enough to accommodate the width of his body, stepped outside quickly, and closed the door behind him. As his hand touched the latch, he had thought he heard the sound of someone moving away from the door, but the suspicion escaped his mind as he looked up at the handsome young ranch hand.

"Yes, sir? May I help you?"

"I hope so. You're Dr. Morris, aren't you?"

"Yes, yes I am. How can I be of assistance? Please make it brief as possible. I'm tending a critically ill patient just now, and it's imperative that I get back to her."

The young man smiled. "I'm real sorry to have bothered you, Doctor, but I've got a bad problem of my own that Lieutenant Kincaid thought you might be kind enough to help me with."

"Lieutenant Kincaid? Of course. What is it?"

"My brother's bad sick with stomach cramps. Must have been something he ate, I guess. Anyway—oh, by the way, my name is Dennis Harper, and Phil is my brother—like I was sayin', he needs some laudanum to ease the pain and help him get into town to see the doctor." He added quickly, "Lieutenant Kincaid told me that you were too busy to go out and see him yourself, so if you could just get some of that painkiller, I'll be on my way."

"Fine, Mr. Harper. Now—"

At that moment, Flora Conway stepped onto the walkway in front of the BOQ with a bundle of linen in her arms. "Good afternoon, Doctor. I've brought a fresh change of bed clothing for the young lady's bed. Would it be all right if I just put them in her room?"

"Good afternoon, Mrs. Conway. That would be fine."

"Good. How is she?"

"Getting better. Much better. At least she's talking now."

"I'm glad to hear that," Flora replied, pushing the door aside and stepping into the room.

Morris glanced over his shoulder at the open doorway, then turned quickly away. "I wish your brother well, Mr. Harper," he said. "Unfortunately, without making a proper diagnosis, I can't prescribe or supply medicine. In the case of stomach cramps, laudanum might not be . . ."

While Morris had been talking, Harper had moved slightly to one side, to make himself clearly visible to the occupant of the room. He made certain that Lee Ellen's eyes met his momentarily, then he turned his gaze back to the doctor. "I guess you're right, Doctor," he said. "I hadn't thought of it that way. I don't know what's wrong with him, and laudanum might be the worst thing for him right now. I reckon I'll just have to cart him into town without it. The town sawbones'll probably be there by the time—"

A piercing scream rattled from the building, followed by Flora's startled shout.

"Doctor! Come quick! She's tearing off her bandages!"

four ————————————

With the sun slipping beneath the horizon, Kincaid
reined in his mount and signaled for the squad strung out behind
him to do likewise. Their search that day had been futile, as
he had suspected it would be, and they had found no sign of
a camp made by one Dennis Harper and his ailing brother,
Phil. While he had originally been given no reason to suspect
any involvement between the man calling himself Harper and
the woman now known as Lee Ellen Dugan, her lapse into near
coma at the mere sight of him, along with his subsequent
disappearance from the post, was sufficient cause to seek him
out for questioning. With night falling, however, he had called
off the search and had paused only to rest their mounts before
returning to the post.

Kincaid rose on his stirrups to step down, but hesitated when the leader of the second squad, Corporal Miller, touched his sleeve lightly.

"Who's that comin', sir?" he asked, pointing in a westerly direction. "Looks kinda like Windy, doesn't it?"

Silhouetted against a blood-red sky, a lone rider loped his mount across the plains; his easy, almost slouched posture in the saddle made the dark outline of man and horse appear to be a single entity.

Kincaid smiled while pushing back his hat. "Sure as hell is. Glad to see the old bastard's on his way home. I hope he knows a little more about what's going on than we do. Have the men dismount and take a break, Corporal. I'll ride out and meet Windy, you wait for me here."

"Yes, sir."

Kincaid heard the order to dismount given as he urged his horse to a gallop and angled toward the still distant rider. As they drew closer to each other, Kincaid saw the heavy Sharps rifle cradled in Windy's left arm, and he thought once again, as he had so often in the past, how fortunate Easy Company was to have Windy Mandalian on its side.

Wearing his ever-present fringed buckskins, with a heavy Walker Colt revolver hanging from one hip and a bowie knife from the other, Windy Mandalian was the embodiment of frontier spirit. His rugged face was dominated by a hawklike nose, and his dark features and taciturn ways might have labeled him as much an Indian as those whom he had fought so many years, both as a trapper and an army scout. There were few, either Indian or white, who wished to cast their lot against him.

Mandalian gave no indication of having recognized Kincaid until their horses were ten yards apart and slowing to a walk. "Evenin', Matt," he said, turning his mount in beside Kincaid's. "Comin' or goin'?"

"I sometimes wonder about that myself, Windy," Kincaid replied with an easy smile, "but in this case we're on our way back to the post. Have any luck at the agency?"

"Depends on whether you mean bad or good, Matt," Windy replied laconically as he carved off a fresh chew of cut-plug, stuffed it in his mouth and chewed on it a bit, then spat before wiping off his knifeblade on a sleeve and shoving it back into the sheath.

"Let's try the good. Seems like we've had plenty of the bad lately."

"Won't take near so long to tell, either. The good luck seems to be that the bad luck ain't started yet."

Kincaid shook his head with a chuckle. "So much for the good luck. Might as well move right along to the bad."

"That's gonna take a mite more tellin', and a whole damned lot more figurin'."

"I assumed as much."

"How many head of beef were supposed to be sent to the Sioux reservation?"

"Two hundred."

"Thought so," Windy allowed with an agreeing nod. "Know how many made it?"

"Half?"

"Nope. Cut that in half, then cut it again."

"Twenty-five head out of two hundred? That won't feed those people for two weeks, let alone the four months it was supposed to."

"I know," Windy replied, scratching his black-whiskered jaw and gazing into the distance. "And worse, the Sioux know it too, and they ain't likin' it one damned bit. When what they've got runs out, word has it that they're done with the talkin' and are gonna get on with the *takin'*. Old Kills Many Bear won't be able to hold 'em back much longer."

"Then at least he's still admonishing them to honor the treaty?"

Mandalian cocked his head sideways with an eyebrow arched. "What's that?"

"Trying to talk them into it."

"That's better. Words like that ain't much different from chewin' the fat part and spittin' out the lean," Windy shifted his cut to the other cheek before continuing. "Yeah, he is but he's up against pretty tough odds. Beaver Claw is probably the most powerful medicine chief those Sioux have, and while he ain't for goin' to war agin the white man, he ain't much for starvin' to death real peaceful-like, either. What we're facing is a test of will betwixt two pretty powerful chiefs. If Kills Many Bear sticks with the terms of the treaty, and things don't work out the way he says they will, he loses face. His medicine is gone. Beaver Claw, on the other hand, will have great medicine and he'll be the new leader of the Sioux. The people seem to be split about fifty-fifty right now as to which chief they stand behind."

Being not unfamiliar with the thought processes of Indians, especially the ferocious Sioux, Kincaid shook his head in obvious concern. "That could be the worst part of all, Windy. If the Indians have no all-out leader, no clear-cut individual in charge, then they could just as easily turn on each other to settle the matter as turn on us."

"For a fact. Medicine means a whole lot of different things, but the one thing it means most is savvy thinkin' and the ability to win, not to mention the actual business of healin' sick people. To them, medicine don't come in bottles and jars. It comes through good rains, winning wars, plentiful game, and a full belly." Windy squinted at the pale evening sky while wiping his mouth with the back of a hand. "Now it don't look to me like it's gonna rain real good again for a while, they lost the last war they fought, there ain't much game left to hunt, and that only leaves one problem that good medicine can solve over bad—the difference 'tween a full belly and an empty one."

"So we're back to the missing beef."

"Yup."

"Did you ever hear of a man called Slater?"

"Has he got a front name?"

"Not that I know."

Windy searched his mind, turned his head to one side and then spat a brown stream of tobacco juice. "Can't help ya, Matt. Might know him, but I can't recall right off. Why?"

"Because his is the only name we've got with regard to the stolen beef. Four days ago, during that heavy rain, Sergeant Olsen and his first squad jumped a bunch of cattle thieves over by Adler's Ravine. Turned out they killed three of them, two white men and a half-breed, and captured a woman who was riding with them. She was shot through the shoulder and damned near died, but in her delirium during the high fever, she kept saying the name Slater every now and then. The funny thing is, though, it seems like she's terrified of him rather than being a willing member of his gang. She mentioned to Dr. Morris—"

"Dr. Morris?"

"Yeah. He came in while you were gone. That's another long story that I'll tell you later over a drink."

"I ain't too wild about the story part, but I'm damned sure ready for that drink. You were sayin'?"

"This Dr. Morris, a green second lieutenant but a first-rate physician, finally got her talking this morning. He wouldn't tell me exactly what she said."

"Why not?"

"His Hippocratic Oath."

"He sounds like a real dandy," Windy replied sardonically. "I can't even remember why I ain't supposed to say something, let alone what not to say."

"Can't hold it against him, I guess. The way he explained it, all doctors are supposed to take that so they can't be used as witnesses against their patients. Be that as it may, he did mention the name Slater, and it had a very dramatic effect on her. He thinks she was about to say he is the one responsible for the rustling—all of it, not just that one bunch. Then this cowboy drifter knocks on the door, a man calling himself Dennis Harper. She sees him and it puts her into some kind of shock and she hasn't said a damned word since. Tried to kill herself after she saw him, as a matter of fact."

Windy tilted his hat forward to scratch the back of his neck. "Let's see now. We've got a strange doctor, a woman with a bullet through her shoulder, three rustlers dead, a man named Slater, and a cowboy drifter who may or may not be named Dennis Harper. You've been busy, Matt. Anything else?"

"Yes, one thing more." Kincaid hesitated before glancing at Windy. "We buried Stoney Jenkins three mornings back. He was killed by the rustlers."

Mandalian's expression turned cold, and they rode in silence for nearly a minute before Kincaid said, "I'm sorry, Windy. I know how much he meant to you. He meant a lot to all of us."

"Yup. Shore did. We've got a man named Slater to find, Matt. I've got me some business to tend to with him. You go ahead on and ride in with your boys now, Matt. I'd like to just kinda mosey on in by myself. Got a little thinkin' to do."

"Sure Windy," Kincaid replied, watching the scout turn away and ride alone across the plains. He knew exactly what was going through Mandalian's mind, and he was extremely glad he wasn't a man named Slater.

"Did ya see her?" Slater asked before Reeves's boot could touch the ground as he stepped down from his saddle.

"Sure did, Slate. And she saw me. Made a point of that. And I can tell you one thing, she's just as scared of you now as she was before. Maybe even more. I don't think she's gonna be tellin' any stories out of school."

Slater grinned and his tongue traced across chipped, uneven teeth. "That's good, Danny boy. You done real good. Did it work the way I said?"

"Yup. Old Shorty was right, they do have their own doctor now, and he's the one that patched up Lee Ellen. I could tell just from the way he acted that he's plumb sweet on her already."

Slater bristled immediately. "Watcha mean by that?"

"Now don't get your dander up, Slate," Reeves said, holding up his hands in mock defense. "That could play right into our hands. Think about it—if she was just another patient, he wouldn't really give much of a shit about her in a personal way. But what if he kind of took a real heavy liking to her? He might be willing to do something real foolish if she got taken away from him, don't you reckon?"

"You got somethin' in mind, Reeves?" Slater asked suspiciously. "If you do, let's hear it."

"Been workin' on it all the way back here," Reeves replied, looping his reins around a broken hitch rail. "If she's gonna help us find that cash once we get those featherheads kickin' shit out of each other, we're gonna have to get her back, aren't we?"

"That's right," Slater growled. "Don't take no goddamned genius to figure that out."

Reeves ignored the burly leader's remark. "And to do that, we're gonna have to get her out of that fort, right?"

"Right, dammit!"

"Well, I was there, and I got a good look at things. A real good look." Reeves paused with a smile, and it was obvious that he was enjoying his leverage over Slater. "And I got it figured how we can get her out. Need a little help from a lovesick doctor maybe, which we'll get, and maybe some cooperation from that photographer we saw yesterday."

"You mean that crazy bastard what was takin' them pictures of that burned-out homestead up near Cannon Spring? What call's he got to help us?"

"He ain't got a reason." Reeves grinned again and added, "Yet."

• • •

"More brandy, Matt? Windy?"

When both men nodded, Captain Conway refilled their glasses then took up the sheets of paper spread across the desk.

"What I have here are the records on stockmen who have contracts with the government to supply beef to agencies within our area. Out of desperation mostly, since we don't have a hell of a lot else to go on except the name, Slater, I requisitioned them from headquarters to try and get a line on trends, anything that might prove out of the ordinary."

"And?" Kincaid asked, looking up over his glass. "Did you find anything worthwhile, sir?"

"I can't tell for sure," Conway responded, taking up his cigar and leaning back in his chair. "Government beef is not branded until after purchase and delivery. For identification purposes, that virtually makes them the original owner's cattle until iron is put to hide. Sometimes, at least according to these records, that takes a week, often two."

"What are you getting at, sir?"

"Mainly that we have no proof of ownership, with the exception of receipts, of course, for a considerable period of time after the sale has been made. Now," he said, blowing out a wisp of smoke while scrutinizing the forms more closely, "one name keeps cropping up here as a major beef contractor for the government, a man named Wes Dobler. According to this, he owns the Flying M spread, and three weeks ago he was consigned forty head of cattle to deliver to the Sioux reservation." Conway glanced up at Kincaid. "How many cattle did Gus estimate were in that herd he came across?"

"Thirty, maybe forty. He didn't have much time for an accurate count."

"I understand that. But it is a little strange, isn't it? Those were Standing Y beef that Gus saw, he remembers that clearly, but they were heading south instead of north, as they should have been. The boys that work these ranges around here don't get lost easily, if you understand what I mean."

"Then what you're saying, Captain, is that—"

"Correction, Matt. Not saying, merely hypothesizing."

"I stand corrected, sir. Your hypothesis, then, is that Standing Y cattle are sold to the government, collected for, and then stolen back again by someone else?"

"Absolutely," the captain replied, glancing across at the scout. "What do you think, Windy? Does it sound feasible?"

"Sounds like a hell of an idea to me, Cap'n," Windy replied. "Shouldn't wear out the merchandise too bad, walkin' 'em to the auction block and then walkin' 'em home again. There's thousands of places around these parts where a small herd of cattle could be held until the pressure is off, and the only way you'd ever find 'em is to stumble across their trail."

"And if they were moved at night, or during a heavy storm," Kincaid threw in, "like that last bunch were, they could be taken back to the home range and set free to roam. Once they mingled in with the other cattle, no one would be the wiser." Then a thought struck him. "But what about those branding irons Gus found? If they're not altering the brands then why carry those heavy irons along?"

Conway dusted an ash from his cigar. "I wondered about that myself, Matt, and, until I came up with the Flying M brand, it didn't make any sense to me either. Then I took a closer look at one of the irons. Looked at straight on, it appeared to be an M with a long leg on either side. The way it's designed, though, only the two legs would touch hide, and if placed directly over the Y, it would make a perfect Flying M. Care to know who the Standing Y brand is registered to?" the captain asked with a twinkle in his eye.

"I'll take a shot at it, Cap'n," Windy offered. "A neighbor of Wes Dobler's. Somebody close enough to where their cattle might naturally mingle."

"Precisely, Windy. Her name is Maude Perkins. The Standing Y brand is registered to her, and she owns the homestead adjacent to the Flying M. She also has contracts with the government, all of which have been delivered and processed, I might add, so I think she's in the clear. But Dobler? Obviously he has to make good on some deliveries, and when he does, he is not losing any Flying M stock, he's simply delivering Standing Y stock that's gone under the hot iron. Then he steals that same amount of Standing Y cattle."

Kincaid rested the rim of his glass against his lips and studied the far wall in silent contemplation.

"Sounds a little farfetched to you, Matt?" Conway asked, then added with a shrug, "It could be. Anyone with a little mathematical background knows that your answer will always be true to your hypothesis, and if your hypothesis is incorrect, so will your answer be. I realize that every conclusion I've drawn so far is based on circumstantial evidence and in no way would stand up in a court of law. But I think the evidence, however circumstantial it may be, is worthy of further investigation."

Kincaid looked up from his reverie. "I'm not troubled by your theory, Captain, not at all. It sounds entirely logical and feasible to me. But one thing does concern me. When you look at the broad view, a rustling operation of this size is pretty small peanuts after one considers the amount of people involved. And the risk is even greater than the potential profit, a fact that seems to be of concern to most criminal minds. It could be that what we're up against is the old 'forest for the trees' adage. There has to be something bigger involved, something that would warrant a medicine war among the Sioux, with attendant military involvement, loss of life, and the risk of hanging or imprisonment. If what you've laid out is correct, and I believe it is, then we've got to find out who would gain the most from the real reason, whatever that is, for this nickle-and-dime larceny against the government."

"Good point. And what is usually the reason?"

"Money, or power, or both."

"Exactly. And that leads us back to Lee Ellen Dugan. She is the only tangible link we have—"

"Just a minute, Cap'n," Windy said, stopping his glass in midair as it moved toward his mouth. "Is that the woman prisoner?"

"Yes, Windy. Why?"

"And you said her name was Lee Ellen Dugan?"

"Yes, I did. Do you know her?"

"Not now, but I might've, years back. Did she happen to say anything about her daddy?"

"Not to any of us. Maybe she mentioned it to Lieutenant Morris, but if she did, it's of no use to us, because he stands firmly behind his Hippocratic Oath."

"To hell with his hiccups and his oaths, Cap'n," Mandalian said quickly, turning to Kincaid. "Can you get that doctor in here, Matt? Right now?"

"Sure, Windy, but like the captain says, he considers anything the woman told him to be privileged information. And even that dribble of information has dried up since she saw that drifter."

"Maybe we can get it flowin' again. Have him brought here, will you, Matt? There might be a link here that we've been

59 ·

missin'. And if we can't get to the bottom of this, whoever wrote that damned oath of his is gonna have a lot of dead people on his hands."

Kincaid stood, opened the door, and poked his head into the orderly room. "Sergeant Cohen? Would you see to it that Dr. Morris is brought here on the double?"

"Yes, sir. I'll get him myself."

"Thanks, Ben."

No more than five minutes had passed before the door opened again and the first sergeant stood to one side. "Lieutenant Morris is here as requested, Captain."

"Thanks, Ben. Send him in."

There was a look of confusion in Morris's eyes as he stepped into the office, and after saluting, his hands immediately went into the pockets of his white, knee-length coat. "You wanted to see me, sir?" he asked in a less-than-confident tone.

"Yes, I did, Lieutenant, and thanks for coming. Dr. Morris, meet Windy Mandalian. Windy? This is Dr. Frederick Morris."

The scout's big, callused hand closed over the narrow, pinkish fingers offered by Morris, and what passed for a cordial smile flitted across Windy's face.

"Pleasure, I'm sure," Windy grunted.

"The pleasure is mine, Mr. Mandalian. I've heard a lot about you. All good, I might add," Morris said with a weak grin as he flexed his hand before shoving it again into his coat pocket.

"Brandy, Doctor?" Conway asked.

"No, thank you, Captain. I don't drink."

"Good for you," the captain replied, freshening his glass and the other two as well. "Windy here is our chief scout, and he's been in the territory longer than any man I know. He would like to ask you some questions, if you don't mind."

"Certainly, sir. But about what? I fail to see how I could possibly be of any assistance to Mr. Mandalian. Our fields of endeavor are quite far removed, at best."

"Not at all, Doc," Windy said, shifting to a more comfortable position against the wall. "I put holes in 'em and you patch 'em up. I've helped to keep a couple of sawbones like yourself in business."

Morris stiffened visibly, and there was a hint of sharpness to his tone. "Perhaps it could be viewed that way, Mr. Mandalian. How can I help you."

"First off, I'd like to know a little bit more about this Hipp—what was that name again, Matt?"

"Hippocratic Oath."

"Yeah, that's it. Without all the fancy trimmin's, tell me what that means."

"Regarding what? It covers a good deal of ground."

"The part about you not bein' able to tell us what your patient said."

"I thought as much," Morris replied, clearing his throat nervously. "Simply stated, whatever is told to me by a patient in confidence, or unbeknownst to that patient, shall remain forever confidential."

"Forever?" Windy asked, massaging the back of his neck. "Now that's a piece of time, ain't it? 'Bout as long as people are dead for, come to think of it."

"That's true. Some secrets are taken to the grave."

"Secrets? Ain't there a difference 'tween secrets and information?"

"In some cases, I suppose. What is your point, Mr. Mandalian?"

"Seems to me that a secret is somethin' somebody tells you with the promise that you won't tell anybody else. But confidential information? Now that's a horse of a different color. That's somethin' somebody tells you because they know somethin' that nobody else is supposed to know, but it ain't real personal, like a secret." Windy's eyes narrowed, and his steely gaze fixed upon Morris's face. "'Cause it ain't personal anymore when that information could save many lives. You are in the life-savin' business, ain't you, Lieutenant?"

"Yes, but I'm not in the information business."

"One and the same, sometimes, Lieutenant. If I held back information that could save your life, and did, then your death would be on my hands, more or less. Not much different from your savin' that woman's life by takin' a bullet out of her shoulder, is it? Just eliminates the middle man, so to speak."

Morris tried to match Windy's intense gaze, but failed and glanced away. "In the strictest terms of logical debate, I would have to agree with you, Mr. Mandalian. But not in terms of doctrine. Besides, your argument can be used against you. What if a doctor were to divulge information that led to his patient's death at the hands of those wishing to see that person eliminated?"

"Then that'd be like puttin' the bullet back in the wound, right enough," Windy allowed.

Kincaid had been listening intently to the conversation thus far, and now he picked up his cue without hesitation.

"You came here with advanced medical knowledge that most doctors aren't even aware of out here, Lieutenant. And you are to be congratulated for your abilities," Kincaid said, speaking evenly, as though he were taking no sides. "You also brought with you a code of ethics that might work very well back on the East Coast, and here as well, in some cases. However, life on the frontier is generally governed by a law dictated by the needs of the many over those of the few. It is called the law of survival, Lieutenant Morris. Oftentimes, for the law to be interpreted correctly, it requires the judgment of several honest men with the best intentions and bound by a sense of duty."

Morris glanced first at Windy and then back at Kincaid. "Are you telling me, sir, that you want me to violate a principle of medicine that has been honored for centuries and is a cornerstone of the medical profession?"

"No. All I'm telling you is that sound judgment often supersedes a strict interpretation of one's own beliefs."

"I am sorry, sir, but I took an oath to uphold certain rules of moral conduct. Therefore, I must refuse to divulge anything Miss Dugan told me that I feel might be an infringement upon my obligation to her as a physician."

Conway stubbed out his cigar and watched the young lieutenant over the smoke rising from the ashtray. "Is that your final word on the subject, Doctor?"

"It is, sir. And I am sorry."

"You believe, then, in the strictest interpretation of the rules, no matter whom they may hurt?"

"I do, sir."

"Fine," Conway said, leaning back again and continuing to speak in a firm, precise tone. "You will be expected to have your medical equipment and personal belongings packed within the hour. And I will expect you to be off this post within that time. Good day, Lieutenant."

Morris's face was frozen in a look of stunned surprise. "What, sir?"

"You heard me, Lieutenant. It is not customary for junior officers to question the judgment of their superiors, and I am not in the habit of repeating myself." Conway took up the set of orders lying on his desk and held them out toward Morris. "Take these with you. You will need them when you arrive at your proper destination."

"Arrive... what... I don't understand, sir. Are you ordering me off this post because I refuse to cooperate with Mr. Mandalian?"

"No. I'm ordering you off this post because you don't belong here. Your duty assignment is Fort McDowell, Arizona, approximately one thousand miles to the southwest. A clerk somewhere along the line made a mistake, which Lieutenant Kincaid discovered. It was my intention to bend the rules a little bit and allow you to remain here to treat the woman until this matter was cleared up, but that is against army regulations. You are, according to *my* oath to obey the laws of this nation, to be directed to your proper assignment immediately. In the strictest interpretation of those guidelines, that means now, Lieutenant. A man with your great fondness for letter-of-law evaluations should certainly be able to understand that."

"But... but... Captain. Lee Ellen—ah, Miss Dugan—needs my care for quite some time yet," Morris said, his words flustered and rapid-fire. "She could well die, sir, if she doesn't receive the proper medical treatment!"

Conway shrugged, then closed his fingers over his chest. "Be that as it may, Lieutenant, the rules are made to be obeyed as written. Have your things packed and be gone within the hour. I can get Dr. Barkley to come out from town and look in on her from time to time."

"Dr. Barkley? He's no doctor, sir! He's a... butcher at best."

"I'm aware of that, but we'll make do and suffer the consequences, as we have in the past. I'll have my personal orders drawn and signed for your continuation to your proper duty assignment by the time you're prepared to leave." Conway reached for his pen and a sheet of paper, and said, without looking up, "Now, if you'll excuse me, Lieutenant, I have work to do."

Morris's beseeching eyes held on the captain for long moments, then went in turn to Kincaid and Mandalian. Kincaid shrugged and Windy merely continued to stare at the lieutenant, who started to turn toward the door, then stopped and gazed at the far wall. The only violation of the silence was the rasping scratch of Conway's steel-nibbed pen across paper. Morris turned slowly to face Windy with half-lowered eyes.

"All right, Mr. Mandalian, I'll tell you what I can," he said in a defeated voice. "What do you want to know?"

"Everything," Windy replied tersely.

Morris nodded and slowly repeated the entirety of his conversations with Lee Ellen.

"Old Dugan and Jake Slater," Windy said softly when Morris had finished speaking.

Matt Kincaid looked up sharply at him. "Do you know this Dugan, then, Windy?"

"'Fraid so," Windy replied. "Or *knew* him, anyways. It was the part about his bein' in prison that tipped me off. Old Dugan and me was good friends at one time. Then after his wife died, he turned drifter and I never saw him again. 'Bout ten years ago I heard that he'd teamed up with some other feller and they knocked over a bank or two. Could be that other feller was this Slater. They finally got caught and sent to prison, but the loot from their last job were never recovered. There was a story goin' around that Dugan hid it somewheres in the territory hereabouts. That money could be the reason we're lookin' for, Matt."

"At least it gives us a place to start," Matt said. "Where were Dugan and Slater captured?"

Windy thought for a moment, then sighed and said, "All this is pretty old stuff, Matt, and I ain't sure how much of it we can trust. If I follow your drift, you're thinkin' that the loot from that last bank job might be hid in the same place where Dugan and Slater was captured, right?"

Kincaid just smiled.

"Thought so," Windy said with a nod. "They was arrested on what's now Sioux land."

"Well, then," Matt said, "I guess we've got our work cut out for us any way you look at it." He turned toward Morris.

"Thank you very much, Lieutenant. We can delay your transfer to Fort McDowell for a while, and it could take from a month to a year for your orders to come back properly drawn." He smiled and guided Morris toward the door by an elbow. "That should give Miss Dugan plenty of time to recover, shouldn't it?"

Morris pumped Kincaid's hand, and his face beamed with satisfaction. "Yes, sir, it sure should, sir. Thank you very much. I'm sorry I gave you so much trouble, but—"

"Don't mention it, Lieutenant. I admire your faith in your convictions. They will serve you well, as long as you don't forget that certain other people are worthy of your trust and confidence. Shouldn't you be getting back to your patient now?"

"Yes, sir. I've been away too long as it is."

"Young feller?" Mandalian said as Morris stepped to the doorway.

"Yes, Mr. Mandalian?"

"Take good care of her, son. I've got a special interest in Lee Ellen's welfare, just like you do."

"You have?"

"Yup, I have," Windy said with a wink. "Just 'cause I ain't seen her in quite a spell, that don't mean I'm not still her godpappy."

five ——————————

Situated as it was upon a great depression in the surrounding prairie, the Sioux village was a picture of tranquility, with yellow flowers dotting the lush, calf-high grass and horses grazing contentedly in the distance. Numerous tipis were scattered across the sloping ground, and the whitish-gray color of hides stretched taut across support poles contrasted with the rich green. Here and there, children darted among tipis at their play, while the women of the Sioux village carried out their daily chores.

But the beauty of the setting was lost on eight men who were seated cross-legged upon the matted grass. The smoke from a dying cookfire situated in their midst drifted lazily into the hard blue sky above. To one side sat Kills Many Bear with three warriors flanking him to his left, and across from him was Beaver Claw, with an equal number of braves by his side. Standing a short distance away and separated from them by a space of thirty yards, two groups of warriors waited in silence while their leaders met in council.

Beaver Claw's eyes strayed from the opposing chief's face, and he watched with a combination of mild interest and unveiled disgust as four squaws artfully skinned a beef hung from a tripod near the meandering stream.

"This is what the white agent sends us, my brother?" he asked, indicating the carcass with a dismissing wave of his hand. "Enough of the white man's cattle to last us no more than a moon, when he has said we would be given enough to last until the coming of the snow?"

Kills Many Bear, his weathered face creased with wrinkles and his hair flecked with gray, didn't bother to glance in the direction indicated, and maintained his constant gaze upon Beaver Claw.

"There is some difficulty. The agent is an honorable man. He has said more will be sent, and we must wait until they are."

"And in this we have another of his many promises?"

"Yes, it is a promise."

"Kah!" Beaver Claw barked, spitting to one side as if to clear a bad taste from his mouth. "I will hear no more of promises. The winter is long, and we must prepare now if our people are to survive."

There was a marked contrast between the two chiefs, but it was not one of dress or habit. Kills Many Bear bore the marks of numerous battles, as did Beaver Claw, and each was dressed in leggings, loincloth, and laced-bone breastplate, and wore twin eagle feathers in their hair. They were both lean men, and even in their advancing years they retained a sinewy ruggedness. There, however, the similarities ended.

Kills Many Bear gave the impression of a man resigned to promises made long ago, treaties signed in good faith. About him there was an air of patience, of commitment to an agreement beyond his ability to reverse. Beaver Claw, on the other hand, was an intense man who tended to lean forward when he spoke, as if by mere force of words he could alter the course of his life and press onward against an increasingly hard wind. Where Kills Many Bear's face was an expressionless mask, Beaver Claw was an animated man, emphasizing his argument with facial contortions and gesticulating hands. Kills Many Bear seldom allowed his voice to rise above a monotone devoid of emotion, and his eyes never wavered as he spoke. With his arms clenched firmly across his chest, he seemed an immovable stone embedded deeply in the earth.

"I have survived many more winters than you, my brother," Kills Many Bear said evenly, "and there is no need to remind me of their length or the need for preparations. But the times have changed, and we must change with them if we are to live. We are no longer free to roam in search of buffalo, as we once were. We must take only what we are given, and if we are given as much as the White Father promised, we will survive."

"Given?" Beaver Claw snapped. "Are we to be like the weak dog who eats only when the strong have finished, and then only the worst of what is left?"

A thin, tight smile pulled at Kills Many Bear's lips. "That is what we have now, the worst of what is left. But to fight again for what we and our ancestors once had would be even more foolish than to try and live as we do now, with the white man's broken promises. We have nowhere to go. Our great chief, Tatanka Yatanka, has found that to be true in Canada. He, like you, Beaver Claw, wanted to live the way things were in the Shining Times before the white man came. But he found Canada to be no home, and the Grandmother across the water no better to him than the White Father to us. He has even less than we do," Kills Many Bear concluded sadly. "He no longer sees the sun set upon the burial ground of his ancestors, nor can he live among the hunting grounds of his people. And worse, he can never return without punishment."

"Punishment?" Beaver Claw asked, his chest swelling as he struck it with a fist. "I fear no punishment from the white man. Beaver Claw has strong medicine, and the gods smile down upon him."

"Yes, you have strong medicine. But our people? Their medicine might not be quite so strong. For warriors, it would be easy to fight the white man and to die proudly with a war lance in hand. But what about them?" Kills Many Bear asked softly, nodding his head toward three young girls playing a hoop game near the stream. "Their hand has not touched the war lance. Are they to die as we would?"

Beaver Claw glanced at the trio, and his face softened momentarily, then became rigid once more. "It would be better for them to die with pride than to live as fish in a stream in which little water flows." His eyes fixed on the elder chief, and they narrowed as he spoke. "You once were a great war leader, Kills Many Bear, and a great leader of our people. Now you are an old woman who feeds from the hand of the white agent."

Kills Many Bear nodded. "That is said by some," he admitted.

The chief's stoic acceptance of the accusation was no surprise to Beaver Claw, but there was something about the confrontation that saddened him, and his powerful physique seemed to droop momentarily.

"We have been friends for many seasons, Kills Many Bear. We have fought and hunted together as one, and now my heart is heavy for this thing that comes between us. What I do, I must do for the sake of our people."

"You are a Sioux warrior. Your decisions are your own."

Beaver Claw took up a twig, which he broke in equal halves with a nod toward the two groups of warriors. "Our people are broken like this stick. This end believes in you and will follow only you," he said, raising his left hand, "and this end will follow me. Those who follow me will leave the reservation to hunt for buffalo on the forbidden hunting ground. If they return with hides and meat, I will be the new chief of our tribe. Our people will know I have strong medicine and they will listen only to me."

"And if they fail?"

"They will not fail. The forbidden hunting ground is where the buffalo now graze, and there are few left on this thing they call a reservation. My warriors will be successful."

"We must have a permit to hunt off the reservation," Kills Many Bear pointed out. "If you hunt without that permit, you will have broken the treaty."

Beaver Claw threw the two sticks into the fire in disgust. "There is no treaty! Only promises the white men will not keep. We will take what we must, hunt in the old way, with lances, and they will not know that we were even there."

"Then you must take the ways of an old woman too?" Kills Many Bear asked. "In the old way, the Sioux did not care who knew they were taking buffalo."

Caught by surprise, Beaver Claw was silent for several moments before standing quickly. "We have talked enough.

My warriors must go now to catch the buffalo when the sun is high in the sky."

Kills Many Bear's eyes drifted slowly to the group of warriors who had placed themselves on the side of an invisible line that put them in league with Beaver Claw. His gaze centered on one tall young man standing in front of the assembly. Lean and powerfully built, he stood there silently, demonstrating no emotion and giving no indication of having noticed the old chief's singular attention upon him.

"Who will lead your hunting party?" Kills Many Bear asked softly, as his eyes once again centered on Beaver Claw.

Beaver Claw met his old friend's solemn stare and said in a distinctly regretful tone, "Striking Hawk. He is the chosen one, but it is not a thing I wish for."

No trace of emotion showed on Kills Many Bear's face. "He is a Sioux warrior, and he must make his own decisions. I wish him, and the others, well." Kills Many Bear rose and walked slowly to the band of warriors waiting in the distance. He stopped before Striking Hawk, stared at him silently for long moments, then reached forward with both hands and clasped the young warrior firmly about the biceps.

"Do what you must, my son. May the gods smile down upon you."

"Have you been down to see her, Windy?" Kincaid asked as the two men led their horses toward the squad mounted and waiting in the center of the parade.

"No, Matt. Not yet. I think I'd better give her a little more time before I stick my ugly face back into her life again."

"Maybe so. When we get back from this patrol will be soon enough, I suppose."

"Yup. Give her a little more time to get a leg under her. If she's in this thing as deep as it appears she is, what we've got to talk about ain't gonna be real pleasant." Windy spat sideways and then wiped off his mouth with his thumb. "Damned shame, too. Last time I seen her, she was a purty little gal with ribbons in her hair. Now she's got a bullet hole in her shoulder. One don't seem quite fittin' with the other."

Kincaid saw Captain Conway angling toward them, and he led his mount several steps in the direction of the telegraph shack. "Good morning, Captain. We're about ready to move out. Any luck with that wire?"

"Morning, Matt, Windy. No luck at all. The sum of their response was that the Sioux have been allocated an ample ration of beef, so there is no need to increase the amount of buffalo they can hunt off the reservation. Besides, they were quite emphatic. They want the Sioux kept on the reservation, not allowed to wander away from it."

"Damned fools," Mandalian muttered. "Takin' their best hunting ground away from them was bad enough, let alone denying them the right to hunt there when needs be. Why weren't those buff wallers up on the north corner of Dobler's property included as part of Sioux land when the reservation was laid out?"

"Because the same people who now deny them additional permits are the ones who drew up the boundaries, Windy. They don't know any better and are too damned smug to ask."

"Figures. The Sioux now call that corner the 'forbidden hunting ground,' and leavin' em starve with buff not far away is like tyin' a mare in heat just out of reach of a stallion, Cap'n. Either they get the cattle they were promised, or they'll take the buff they feel is rightfully theirs in the first place."

"I know that, Windy. That's why I want you and Matt to take this patrol. We've got a lot riding on its outcome." Now Conway turned to Kincaid. "Matt, I know Dobler is going to raise hell, but I want you to tell him about our problem with getting beef to the Sioux, as if he doesn't already know. Tell him we'll expect another one hundred and seventy-five head delivered within the week. While you're having a conversation with him, Windy will circulate among Dobler's stock and see if he can't match some fresh brands up with that iron we were talking about the other day. If he does, maybe we can catch Dobler at his own game."

"He'll raise hell, no doubt about that, sir. And he'll demand additional payment as well."

"Stall him. Say the voucher is being processed, held up in channels somewhere, anything to convince him that this is a legitimate requisition from the Bureau of Indian Affairs."

"I'll do it, sir," Kincaid replied, touching boot to stirrup and swinging easily into his saddle. "What if Windy finds those fresh brands you mentioned? We don't have enough evidence to convict him of rustling, because he'll just deny any involvement with Slater. I don't think placing him under arrest at this time will help us any."

"No, don't arrest him. Just pass along the request for more beef, have a look around, then come back here and let me know the outcome. We'll make our next move from there."

"Fine, sir. We should be back by tomorrow noon at the latest."

"Good. Have a safe patrol. Swing by and talk to Stearns on your way back, and fill him in on what's been going on. He's not in a very good position right now, if the Sioux decide to break the treaty."

"I'll do that, sir. Corporal! Let's move out!"

Striking Hawk could not have felt more full of life, free, and powerful than he did at that exact moment. Since the days of his youth he had seen the initiated warriors of the tribe return from raids and battles brandishing scalps, weapons, clothing, and other possessions taken from fallen enemies. They had always been inflamed with a sense of wild fulfillment, as though warfare, the ultimate test of courage, had brought them to the peak of their existence and victory had provided them that one exhilarating moment for which fighting men lived and were prepared to die. And there was a pungent odor about them that would forever live in his nostrils: the smell of burned gunpowder, blood, sweat, and dust all captured and contained in the rancid, somewhat sweetish smell of bear grease and warpaint.

Then there were the war ponies, much like the one between Striking Hawk's legs at that very moment. Wild-eyed and skittish, they pranced with regal pride. Along with the other boys his age, it had been Striking Hawk's responsibility to cool off those mounts before walking them in the stream, and more than once he had leaped upon the back of a mighty war pony and raced across the plains in pursuit of an imaginary enemy.

But the most unforgettable sight of all had been that of his father, riding at the head of the war party and always the one who had taken the most scalps, braved the greatest risks, and led his warriors home again in glorious victory. As a boy he had stood at the head of his father's mount while waiting for him to leap to the ground with bloodied spear brandished aloft, and he'd dream of the day when he would be the one who led his people in battle. But shortly after passing his manhood ritual, what Striking Hawk envisioned as his future suddenly became the past and there were no more raids or battles. The treaty with the whites had been signed and there was no more war with the Arapaho, the Cheyenne, or the Crow. His people were now told where to live, what to hunt and where, and given strange food to eat. At the bursting point of youth blossoming into manhood, Striking Hawk had been told to lay his war club aside and accept a confined life within the boundaries of the reservation. Tests of strength with his contemporaries, at which he always excelled, were not enough to restrain the warrior's heart beating in his breast, and he had begun to listen more keenly to the rhetoric of those opposed to his father's attempted compliance with the white man's wishes.

Even though he was untested in battle, he was not unfamiliar with the look of hurt and betrayal that he had seen in his father's eyes when their arms had clasped no more than an hour before. But the driving force that compelled him to take up the lance in opposition to his father's counsel was too great, too strong even for the bonds of filial commitment to contain. During moments alone on the great prairie with a pony between his legs that had never carried him to battle and a lance in his hand that had never drawn enemy blood, Striking Hawk had wondered what he was to tell his children. That Striking Hawk, son of the great chief Kills Many Bear, lived his life wearing the white man's rags, eating the white man's food, and was not warrior enough to provide for his own family? If he was among the last, so be it, but he, Striking Hawk, would be known as a Sioux warrior who hunted and fought and killed in the ways of his ancestors and a man whom the gods would welcome as a fitting leader of his people.

Feeling the wind brush across his face and hearing the solid thud of galloping hooves tearing into sod behind him, Striking Hawk contained the urge to turn and scream a war yell at the twenty other young braves strung out to the rear. A war chief showed no emotion until the battle had been won, and Striking Hawk grasped the lance more tightly in his hand and concentrated on the horizon. Buffalo for the cooking fires had been dismissed from his mind, and he envisioned countless Crow warriors waiting just beyond the next rise and now trembling in fear at the prospect of facing the mighty Sioux in battle.

At the sound of hoofbeats striking the packed earth in the yard before the house, Wes Dobler leaned back in his chair, pulled a watch from his vest pocket, and checked the time. One-fifteen. After one final glance at the ledger spread before him, he yawned, splashed a measure of whiskey into the glass beside his elbow, and drank deeply as he heard the pounding of boots on the porch steps. He was a man of medium build, neatly dressed and wearing a carefully tended mustache that seemed to lessen the unsightliness of his pockmarked face. Even though he combed his straight black hair down alongside his temples, its thickness was not sufficient to conceal the fact that half of his left ear had been cut away, leaving a scar that he unconsciously caressed with a thumb when in thought. Dobler swiveled his chair to face the man standing in the doorway, and there was a deep, almost hateful glitter in his dark eyes.

"Sorry to bother ya, boss," the paunchy, elderly ranch hand said as he wiped his mouth in a nervous motion. "But I think we might have some trouble brewing up in the northeast corner."

Dobler's eyes narrowed to slits. "What kind of problems? You know I've told you and everyone else to stay the hell away from there unless it's damned important."

"I know that, boss, and we do. But I can't say the same for a bunch of featherheads."

"Featherheads? Are there Indians on our side of the line?"

"Not just yet, exactly. But they're headed our way. Linker saw 'em, and he said it looked like twenty, maybe thirty at most."

"How are they armed?"

"Linker said all he could see was lances."

Dobler's thumb went to the scar and he turned slowly toward the desk in thought. "Sounds like a hunting party, and if it is, they're probably on the way to those damned buffalo wallows." He spun again toward the hired hand and snapped, "How many of the boys are down at the bunkhouse?"

"Ten. The other two was with me and Linker, uh . . . doin' that job you told us to do."

"Good. Get your ass back to the bunkhouse and tell the boys that I want every man armed to the teeth and mounted within ten minutes. If those Indians take one damned buffalo from our side of the line, I want to be there when they do. That property is mine, and every damned head of anything that's on it belongs to me. It's about time I taught those Sioux a little lesson about taking something that belongs to Wes Dobler." He allowed a tight, wicked smile to twist the corners of his thin lips. "Besides, it isn't right to steal. Especially from your neighbors. Now move it, Ward! Tell Brock to stay behind in case something goes to hell around here."

"Right, boss. Been a long time since I had an Injun in my sights," he said with a wistful grin as he turned away.

"You will have today, if they cross over," Dobler replied, waiting until the hired hand moved away before turning again to the ledger, which he carefully opened to the last page. Gingerly, as if touching fragile parchment, he took up a half sheet of paper in his fingertips and turned it to the light. The document was soiled and deeply creased from years of folding and unfolding, and its edges were worn ragged. Dobler's finger traced the symbols drawn on the paper, and then followed twin intersecting lines that stopped three inches apart at the torn crease that had been the center of the page.

"Damn," he muttered, staring into the space that would have been the other half of the map. "It's got to be around there somewhere, but where? Is it on the reservation side, or my side? Slater had one half and Dugan had the other. Now Dugan's dead and Slater thinks his daughter has the missing section. We're fucked without that piece, and Slater's supposed to have brought her here by now. Damn him anyway," Dobler hissed through gritted teeth as he carefully tucked the map back into its hiding place. "I'll see him tonight when we pick up those cattle, and he damned well had better come up with the right answers. I've been more than ten years waiting for this, and I've put up with enough ranching bullshit to last me a lifetime."

Rising, Dobler carefully placed the ledger in a heavy black safe, closed the door quickly, and twisted the dial several times, then put on his hat and reached for his gunbelt, which was hanging from a wall peg.

"Until then, the last thing I need is for a bunch of Injuns to be stumbling around up there," he said, adjusting the belt to his hips and moving toward the door. "A dead brave or two, killed during a surprise attack by them, of course, should do the trick. I've got a right to protect my own property, and there isn't a hell of a lot the army can do about that."

Striking Hawk had felt it earlier in the day, but had dismissed the sharp pain just to the inside of his right hipbone as nothing more than a slightly strained muscle. But he had felt it several more times during the ride to the wallows, and now, as he sat

76

on his pony just beneath the crest of the last rise, he felt dizziness sweep over him, with accompanying nausea. Just moments before, he had felt extremely warm and then suddenly chilly. A slight film of perspiration formed on his upper lip, and his skin felt clammy and cold. He closed his eyes, gritted his teeth, and bent over sharply with another stabbing flash of pain.

"Are you all right, my brother?" asked the brave nearest to Striking Hawk. "You look as if a hot knife had been pressed against your side."

Striking Hawk glanced up quickly and shook his head to clear his vision. The sun was a brilliant, searing yellow ball in the sky, and his companion swam before his eyes like a shimmering mirage.

"Yes, I am all right," Striking Hawk managed, striving to conceal his agony with a disarming smile. "The white man's meat does not agree with me."

"The forbidden hunting ground is before us, Striking Hawk," the warrior replied, motioning with his lance toward the crest. "We will have our own food on the fires when the sun has vanished. We should strike now while the buffalo have full bellies and are ready for sleep."

"Yes, I know," Striking Hawk said, feeling the anger rise from deep within in response to the pain that threatened to steal this moment of glory from him. Determination welled within his mind, and he forced himself to sit straight upon the pony's back. "We will strike now. I will take the lead bull. I expect each warrior to bring down at least one animal."

Striking Hawk glanced away to hide the grimace crossing his face, then lashed his moccasined heels against the horse's flanks and bent low to its neck as the animal broke into a gallop. Holding the tip of his lance low above his horse's front shoulder, he crested the rise at a dead run, with his companions racing close behind.

With the exception of a few cows and calves wandering aimlessly about, nuzzling the tall grass for tender spring morsels, the majority of the herd were bedded down in the cool dust of the wallows, content to doze through the heat of the day. Until Striking Hawk's yell split the stillness, they were unaware of the enemy bearing down on them from above. Their shaggy heads swung in unison toward the sound as they lurched forward on stubby front legs and bolted upright in a flurry of

77

switching tails and clouds of dust. By the time they had stumbled into a gallop, Striking Hawk's mount had already penetrated their ranks and was knifing toward the lead bull, which had, in a relatively short distance, achieved startling speed for an animal so strangely designed.

Mindless of the burning pain in his side, the young warrior concentrated on his prey and guided his horse forward at a closing angle, while locking the heel of the lance between his inner arm and the right side of his chest. Sunlight glinted off the blade, which had now passed the animal's bald rump and was aimed directly at a point just below the hump and behind its left shoulder. His pony was rapidly outdistancing the buffalo, and Striking Hawk leaned forward and slightly down as the kill spot came into view, then slammed the blade home and watched the weapon sink into flesh before it was torn from his grasp with a twisting jolt. He saw the curved, ridiculously small horns on the great animal's head dip forward as the front legs buckled, and from the corner of his eye he saw the rear hooves flailing empty air as the buffalo pitched forward in a tumbling roll.

He jerked backward on the hackamore and pulled his pony into a tight turn as he glanced over his shoulder and saw the shaggy beast flop onto one side with the shaft of the lance protruding just in front of the rib cage while its legs twitched in one final convulsion. He shook his fist and screamed a triumphant war yell as he raced toward the buffalo once more and leaned down to jerk his lance free. Then a blinding pain exploded in his side and he slid from his pony's back to sprawl across the dead buffalo in the same instant that the first booming shot echoed across the plains. More weapons fired simultaneously, and the other young warriors, startled by the unexpected attack, broke off the hunt and whirled their rearing, plunging mounts in wild confusion while two more warriors were slammed from their ponies in instant death.

"How many ya want, boss?" Ward asked, looking up from his sights while a wisp of smoke drifted lazily from his gun barrel.

"Let's see what they do," Dobler replied. "We got their leader and two others. The rest are still out of range. You fired too damned soon."

"Sorry, boss. Guess we got a little anxious. But we can take the whole damned bunch if you want. They ain't got nothin' but spears."

"Yes, and the minute we go for them, they'll hightail it back to the reservation, and we can't go after them there. You know that as well as I do. Look," Dobler said with obvious disgust, "you didn't even kill the son of a bitch you shot."

Ward looked toward the fallen Indian and saw him turn onto his back, then slide down to lean against the buffalo's side in a sitting position. His head was clearly visible, even though it lolled to one side and he was obviously in great pain."

"I'll finish him," Ward replied, raising his Winchester and settling the stock against his shoulder, while his eyes lowered again to the sights. "Don't figure he'll have much yip left in him with his head gone."

Dobler pushed the gun barrel down and away with one hand. "Leave him be. If he lives, I want him to take a message back to his people for me. Come on," he concluded, urging his horse forward, "I want to get up close enough so he can hear me real good."

The last of the buffalo had thundered out of sight and the braves had gathered in a small band a hundred yards from Striking Hawk, where they watched the white men approach with weapons cocked and ready to fire. Knowing they were helpless against repeating rifles, they watched stoically from a distance as Dobler reined in his mount possibly twenty yards from where Striking Hawk lay.

"Hey, Injun! You hear me over there?" Dobler yelled, rising on his stirrups and crossing his hands over the saddle horn.

Striking Hawk turned his upper body with visible effort and twisted his head to stare over his shoulder. "I hear you," he replied, his words strained but showing no fear.

"That's good. Real good. 'Cause I want you to listen, and listen good. This isn't Injun land. It belongs to me, Wes Dobler, and I don't want to ever catch your red ass around here again. Is that understood?"

"You own nothing," Striking Hawk said evenly.

"I don't, huh? I've got homestead rights on part of it, and the rest I bought free and clear with my own money. I own everything on this land, including that buffalo you just killed, and if any of your people trespass on my ground again, they're going to be just as dead as that animal you're leanin' against. I should kill you right now, as a matter of fact, but I'm gonna let you live so's you can set your people straight. You understand that, Injun?"

"You own nothing. The land belongs to the gods, and the

buffalo belong to the land," Striking Hawk replied, straining to keep any sign of pain from his voice.

"Listen to that sass, boss," Ward said, caressing the trigger beneath his finger. "Let me put one more in him. That's the only lesson they understand."

"No, he's wounded bad enough so he won't forget, and neither will his people. We'll let the others take him back, along with the two dead ones over there." Then Dobler raised his voice in Striking Hawk's direction once again. "We'll back off a ways so your thievin' friends can come and get you! Leave that spear of yours where it is and get your ass off my property! You've got five minutes, and no more!"

With that, Dobler turned his horse and led the cattlemen a safe distance away before turning again to watch a lone warrior ride forward, leap down, and help the young warrior chieftain to his feet while the bodies of the dead braves were loaded across their ponies' backs by the other Sioux. Then, with Striking Hawk supported by a brave on either side, the band of warriors rode slowly toward the crest of the prairie swell and vanished from view in the direction of the reservation. When he was sure they had gone, Dobler turned to his men.

"Willy? I want you and Henson to pull that lance out of that dead buff and bring it here. I've got a little job for you to do with it."

"What kind of job, Wes?" the man named Henson asked.

"Find a beef of mine around here somewhere, throw a rope around it, drag it over here, and put a bullet through its shoulder about where the spear is in the buff. Then shove that lance in good and deep. The army will be coming around to investigate what's gone on here. I want 'em to find a dead Flying M cow with a Sioux war lance sticking out of its hide when they do." Again, Dobler grinned with cold satisfaction. "A man's got a right to protect his stock from thievin' Injuns."

six ‾‾‾‾‾‾‾‾‾‾‾‾‾‾‾‾

"Hello the house!" Kincaid called, studying the silent building and then allowing his gaze to drift over the apparently abandoned outbuildings of the rundown homestead. A wagon tilted to one side on its broken axle, corral fences were badly in need of repair, and patches of sunlight could be seen through ancient holes in the barn roof, but there was no sign of activity and the afternoon heat seemed to have driven all living things to the coolness of shaded sanctuaries. A windmill with several blades missing creaked in slow rotations on the ample breeze, and that one grating violation of the stillness caused an eerie sensation to pass through Kincaid's mind and made him think of Windy Mandalian with some concern. Not two hours before, the scout had split off from the remainder of the platoon once they had crossed the boundary onto Flying M land, and he was alone somewhere now, seeking to match fresh brands with the branding iron Captain Conway had examined the previous day.

It was highly unusual for a working cattle ranch to be totally abandoned at midafternoon, and his awareness of that fact caused Kincaid to rise up on his stirrups for a better look around as he said with flat military authority, "Anybody in that house? If so, come out and come out now! This is Lieutenant Kincaid, United States Army! Official business!"

Again, silence, accented by the groaning protestations of a wheel turning on a dry hub. Kincaid turned in his saddle toward the squad waiting patiently behind him, and nodded to Corporal Wojensky. "Have the men dismount and search the out-buildings."

"Yes, sir," the corporal replied, and Kincaid heard his orders being relayed as he stepped from his saddle, mounted the steps of the porch, and depressed the front door latch. He pushed the door open on resisting hinges and stood there for a moment before stepping into the musty room, which was littered with discarded objects and was obviously not the pride of a housewife's eyes. He noticed the littered desk, the whiskey bottle and tin cup, and then the black safe, which he crossed to and observed with mild interest before reaching down and pushing on the oblong lock handle, which was unyielding. Kincaid started to pull his hand away, but when he did, the safe's door opened a crack and he stared at it momentarily. Obviously, whoever had been the last to use the safe had twisted the dial in the assumption that the door was securely closed, and they must not have taken the time to make sure.

Kincaid opened the door slowly and saw a cord hanging from the bottom of the safe, which had prevented a sealing closure. He stopped to pick up the string, which was attached to an empty money bag. He turned the bag to the light and studied the faded printing on one side, but all he could make out were three badly faded words, one of which was partly illegible:

BANK Of   ASTLE

Thoughtfully he hefted the sack in his hand for a moment before returning it to the floor of the safe, with its draw cord hanging out as before. Then he took out the wide ledger, which resembled a paymaster's journal. Kincaid opened the book randomly to a center page and ran a finger down the column of figures delineating cattle sold and purchased, then flipped to another page, which gave account of various business transactions normal to ranch operations. After checking several more pages, Kincaid closed the ledger again and started to return it to the safe, then hesitated. There was something totally incongruous about the neatly detailed, accurately drawn figures in the book and the general clutter of the Flying M homestead.

Kincaid knew it to be true almost without exception that men who worked with figures were fastidious by nature and were generally quite disturbed by any sort of disarray. It was as if they saw themselves personally represented in the neat, orderly columns of numbers, and a digit out of place, or an ink blot, was not dissimilar to a button undone or a hat worn at an odd angle. Obviously, whoever maintained the ledger was either entirely out of his element on the Flying M, or he was so consumed by his project that violations of his personal sense of neatness passed unnoticed. Kincaid opened the ledger again and searched out the initials at the bottom of each column: W. D., written in crisp, tight letters.

Kincaid looked about him, trying to understand the thinking of Wes Dobler, but with little success. The rancher continued to be an enigma, and after nearly five minutes of silent speculation, Kincaid turned, laid the ledger on its shelf, and closed the safe door, leaving it exactly as he had found it. Then he heard Wojensky call from outside.

"Lieutenant? We found a live one, sir! He was down in the barn!"

"Coming, Corporal," Kincaid replied, glancing around the room one final time before stepping onto the porch and closing the door behind him. He adjusted his hat as he descended the steps and his eyes went to an elderly, narrow-shouldered man standing between two privates.

"What's his name, Corporal?"

"Won't say, sir. We found him hiding in the hayloft."

"Hiding?"

"Yes, sir. He says he was takin' a nap, but he was mighty damn awake when he came at us with a pitchfork."

"I see," Kincaid replied, pulling off his right glove as he stopped before the ranch hand. "My name is Lieutenant Kincaid. Do you know where we might find Mr. Dobler?"

"I ain't got nothin' to say to you bluebellies," the man snarled in a heavy Southern accent as he spat to one side.

"Bluebellies, huh?" Matt said with a casual smile. "Army of the Confederacy?"

"You damn bet your boots. Tennessee Regular, I was."

"I see. Good outfit. Topnotch. Some of the best fighting men in the War for the cause of the South. What's your name?"

Disarmed by Kincaid's casual, laudatory remark, the man came to rickety attention and said, "Brock, suh. Toby Brock."

"Pleased to meet you, Mr. Brock. How long have you worked for Mr. Dobler?"

"Ever since I come out West, suh," Brock replied, shifting his weight to his other foot. Kincaid noticed a lessening of height, which would indicate a limp.

"Were you wounded in the War, Mr. Brock?"

"Yup, I was. Took a ball in the right knee at Antietam. Been kind of stove-up ever since."

"That's too bad. It's a shame to see a good soldier put out of action by what must have been a lucky shot."

"Damned right it was, suh," Brock replied instantly, with a hint of forgotten valor lighting up his eyes. "Damned Yank took me whilst I was havin' my mornin' constitutional. Weren't fer that, he'd never a' laid a sight on me."

"I don't imagine he would have, Mr. Brock," Kincaid allowed seriously. "What do you do for Dobler?"

Brock shrugged his sloping shoulders disinterestedly. "Dig, mostly."

"Dig?"

"Yup, that's what I said. Dig here, dig over yonder, wherever he points the shovel. Don't never know what I'm diggin fer, just get paid to dig."

"That's rather strange, isn't it? I didn't realize that Mr. Dobler had mining interests."

Sensing that he had said too much, Brock immediately squared his shoulders and glowered at Kincaid. "Ol' Toby Brock ain't never been one much fer talkin' to the enemy, suh, which I figure you rightly are. I got nothin' else to say."

"I can understand that," Kincaid replied. "But I would like to know where I might find your senior in command. I'm here on official military business. Even though you can't reveal any military secrets, you are at liberty to allow me to make a legitimate proposal to your superior officer under a flag of truce."

"What kinda proposal, suh?" Brock asked suspiciously with an arched eyebrow.

"Come now, Mr. Brock. You know military protocol as well as I do. These matters are to be discussed only between soldiers of equal rank. Where might I find Mr. Dobler?"

Brock studied his mind and nudged a pebble with the toe of his boot as he struggled for a decision. "Guess it wouldn't hurt none fer me to tell ya that."

"Of course not. He is a reasonable man, is he not?"

"Can't rightly say for shore," Brock replied, pushing his rumpled hat forward to scratch the thinning gray hair at the back of his head. "He ain't no possum up a tree, I know that fer true. Kinda strange feller, keeps mostly to hisself an' don't give a damn whuther cows fly or walk. Seems to favor figures and diggin', mostly."

"I see. Well, then, I would be grateful if you'd be so kind as to tell me where I might find him."

"Him an' the other boys cut a trail fer the nawtheast cawner 'bout two o'clock this afternoon. Ol' Ward said somethin' 'bout some Injuns crossin' over to Mr. Dobler's ground, an' they was goin' after 'em. Tol' me to stay here and keep a eye on things, which I was doin' till you fellers showed up."

"The northeast corner?" Kincaid asked quickly. "Are you familiar with that area?"

Brock gave a deprecating chuckle. "Familiar? Hell, suh, I done looked at ever' rock and shovelful of dirt what's ever growed up thar. Familiar ain't the word for it. I know that ground like the wart on Aunt Molly's nose."

"Is that where the buffalo wallows are? Close to the Sioux reservation?"

"Sure 'nuff," Brock replied, obviously pleased with possession of knowledge beyond that of the tall, handsome army officer towering above him. "With a strong wind and a good spit, ya could reach one from t'other."

"Thank you, Mr. Brock," Kincaid replied, pulling on his glove again and turning to Wojensky. "Have the squad mounted and prepared to move out immediately, Corporal. We may be too late already."

"Yes, sir. Mount up, form ranks, and prepare to move out!"

As the soldiers ran toward their horses, the old man watched them with a wistful eye before looking again at Kincaid. "Kinda miss that, yes I do, suh. Guess it's still the same, no matter what the color of the uniform."

"Yes, it is, Mr. Brock. You've been most helpful, and I thank you." Kincaid hesitated, then added, "From one soldier to another."

The old man looked at Kincaid for long moments, his eyes

misted over, then he glanced away. "Thank you, suh. Respect don't come easy these days. You mentioned bein' maybe too late already—mind if I ask what you're too late for?"

"Preventing a war, Mr. Brock," Kincaid replied gently. "Somehow it's more rewarding to prevent one than to win one."

"Wouldn't know about that, suh. Never won one."

"No, I guess you haven't," Kincaid said, starting to move away before seeing the old man's right arm start to rise upward. He stopped, turned back, and returned Brock's arthritic salute with a crisp one of his own.

"Thank you, suh," Brock said softly. "The get-up-and-go might die in an old man's body, but the soldier in him don't."

"Some things can't be taken away, Mr. Brock," Kincaid said. "You must have been a good one."

The old man winked and his face twisted in a wry grin. "Only difference 'tween bein' what I am and what I coulda been was a mornin' shit, suh. Might think about that next time ya get the urge."

"I will, Mr. Brock. Believe me, I will."

With the sun poised for its evening plunge toward the horizon, Kincaid raised his right hand to halt the twin columns and have one final look across the broad landscape in search of Dobler and his ranch hands. They had heard no firing, seen no sign of battle, and Matt was a bit worried that the long search had turned up nothing. With one hand shielding his face from the lowering sun, he strained his eyes in an attempt to pick out some telltale object that would give them a bearing, but the vast prairie yielded no secrets. Then, just as he was about to turn away, a black dot materialized on the horizon and grew rapidly to the proportions of a man and a horse moving toward them at high speed. Kincaid's focus centered on the man, and in less than a minute he recognized the approaching rider as Windy Mandalian.

"Have the men dismount, Corporal," he said over his shoulder, without taking his eyes off the scout. "Windy's coming, and we'll rest the horses here while we wait for him."

"Yes, sir. Disss . . . mount!"

Nearly two minutes passed before Mandalian reined his sweat-lathered horse in besides Kincaid's.

"Afternoon, Matt, I was kinda hopin' I'd cut across your trail. Lookin' for Dobler?"

"Yes, and for you as well."

"Me?" Windy asked with a chuckle. "Hell, Matt, that's like reachin' in your pocket and tryin' to pull out a handful of dark."

"I know that, but I am kind of concerned. I went by Dobler's place as we'd planned, but the ranch was deserted and I didn't find out a hell of a lot. The only person there was an old Reb who was more interested in refighting the Civil War than in giving much help."

"Them Rebs don't lose real good," Windy allowed, reaching for his cut-plug, then changing his mind.

"No, they don't. Anyway, he said something about Dobler taking all his hands and coming up this way because of some Indians crossing onto his land. We've been looking for him since, but with no luck."

"Naw, and you won't have, either," Windy said, squinting toward the east. "I've been trailin' him and about fourteen hands for the last couple of hours or so. Headed over yonder, and I finally gave 'er up to come back and find you."

"Fourteen hands?" Kincaid asked sharply. "What the hell would he be doing with fourteen men, heading away from his home buildings with night coming on?"

"Nice-sized bunch of men to push a herd of stolen cattle on a night drive, Matt," Windy said with a speculating squint of one eye.

"You were pushing your horse pretty hard when you rode up here. Is that the reason?"

"Nope," the scout replied, changing his mind once more and slicing off a chunk of cut-plug, which he nestled in a corner of his cheek. "We've got bigger problems on our hands than stolen cattle."

"Like what?"

"Like war, Matt," Mandalian said softly. "Dirty, mean, blood-red war."

"Between who?"

"Don't know for sure. Maybe between us and the Sioux, with Dobler and his bunch somewhere in between."

"Let's hear it, Windy. What have you got?"

"I came across the northeast corner of Dobler's property 'bout three, maybe four o'clock this afternoon—just after he left, I figure. I heard one lone shot, and that's what brought me over this way."

"One shot? Not much of a battle if there was one."

"There was, and there wasn't. I found a dead buff, killed

in the traditional Sioux way, lance behind the shoulder. The lance was gone, but about fifty yards away there was a dead steer with a Sioux war lance still in its shoulder. Another thirty or forty yards back toward the rise, the grass is covered with blood in two different places. A couple of men must've been shot earlier and either killed or badly wounded."

"Could they have been Dobler's men?"

"Don't think so. I got myself a real good look at the whole damned bunch, and there weren't any empty saddles and nobody was ridin' hurt."

Kincaid contemplated the alternatives for several seconds before asking, "Then you think they were Sioux?"

"Yup. I'm sure of it. There were moccasin tracks in one of the buff wallers where two of 'em had crossed, draggin' a third. 'Sides that, a feather had been dropped, and it was dyed red and yellow, the Sioux war colors."

"All right, we've got two Indians either killed or wounded, one dead buffalo, and a dead steer with a war lance stuck in its heart. Now let's try to reconstruct what happened," Kincaid said as he gazed toward the horizon. "Maybe a group of young warriors took it upon themselves to cross the reservation line and take a few buffalo, and just for the hell of it, one of them puts a lance into a steer. Dobler and his men ride up, see the dead beef, and jump the Sioux. A fight develops; two Indians are wounded, the other braves take them back to the reservation, and Dobler thoroughly riled by now, goes off to check his other stock." After a moment's hesitation, he glanced across at Mandalian with a weak grin. "That sounds a little limp, doesn't it?"

"Yup. Sure does. 'Specially when you keep in mind the fact that the steer wasn't killed by a lance."

"It wasn't?"

"Nope." Windy worked the cut several times, spat, and then added, "The buff was, but I'll bet you a dollar to a cow turd that the steer wasn't."

"What makes you so certain?"

"Since the animal is usually runnin' and has to be caught from behind," Windy explained, "the lance tip goes in at an angle, cuttin' hide as it does, just like on that dead buff. I checked that just to make sure. But the lance went into the steer straight from the side."

"Wait a minute, Windy," Kincaid said. "Maybe the brave just sneaked up on the steer."

88

Windy shook his head. "Not likely, Matt. And there's somethin' else. I suspicion the steer was shot before the lance was shoved into its hide."

Matt's eyebrows rose. "How can you tell about a thing like that?" he asked. "Did you dig the slug out of its hide?"

"Didn't have to," Windy replied patiently.

"How, then?" Kincaid asked expectantly, marveling once again at the uncanny shrewdness of his chief scout.

"Because the lance came out too easy when I pulled on it. The muscle tightens up when the blade goes in, and if the critter has laid there for a while like that one had, it'd take two strong men or more to pull it out. 'Sides, it'd already done its work for one day."

"What do you mean by that, Windy?"

"It was the same lance that killed the bull buff," Mandalian replied with a slow smile. "The steer was white and tan, and the hair matted on the blood around the shaft of the lance was long and dark brown. Buff hair it was, Matt—long and stringy."

"Well I'll be damned," Kincaid said. "Then Dobler is trying to implicate the Sioux by making it look like he was doing nothing more than protecting his own property. Since he had all his ranch hands with him, he must have known they were coming and he had some reason for lying in wait. Some reason other than mere trespass."

"That's the way I see it," Windy replied with an agreeing nod. "Something big enough to risk an all-out raid by the Sioux in retaliation. When some of their own are killed, with no scalps brought back in return, they can get downright nasty, as you know. And they don't just get mad, Matt—they get even."

"Then we are looking at an all-out war."

"We are. If there are some dead, the Sioux'll take a couple of days to make sure the spirits get a proper sendoff to the Happy Hunting Ground, then they'll set about liberating some spirits themselves. Remember, the treaty has been broken, the way some of 'em see it anyway, by our not delivering the cattle promised, and now two braves have been shot for killin' buffalo on ground that they still consider rightly theirs in the first place. Add to that the fact that there's a power struggle goin' on 'tween Kills Many Bear and Beaver Claw, and you've got a kettle of fish that ain't real pleasin' to the nose."

"There's got to be a key to this somewhere," Kincaid said.

"Sombody stands to gain by riling the Sioux up and instigating their return to the warpath, which would naturally involve us. We know about a man named Slater, we've got a prisoner who might or might not have been an accomplice in the rustlings, and Dobler now comes into the picture, not only because of that branding-iron theory of the captain's, but more importantly because of what went on here today. What he did is the same as an attempted frameup, and usually the person principally involved in that sort of thing has a motive either of revenge or personal gain."

Windy adjusted the Sharps to a more comfortable position in the crook of his arm, spat, and then said, "The man who baits the trap checks the trap, Matt. I wonder if them holes up yonder have anything to do with it?"

"What holes?"

"All over the damned place," Mandalian replied with a nod toward the northeast corner of Dobler's property. "Somebody's been diggin' around up there like they lost their grampaw's spectacles. Ain't lookin' for fishin' worms, I'll tell ya that for a fact."

The conversation with Brock came immediately to Kincaid's mind, but revealed no clue as to why the holes had been dug. "I met the man who dug the holes, Windy," Kincaid replied, "and since he hasn't found what he's been looking for yet, that means it's still buried out there somewhere. Maybe we'll be there when he finds it. We'd better get over to the agency and check with Stearns. He's in a bad situation right now if the Sioux do go on the warpath."

"The word ain't 'if,' Matt. It's 'when.' We've got two days or less, dependin' on how fast spirits fly."

It was after dark when Wes Dobler pulled up and dismounted before the sod cabin. Jake Slater stood on the porch with a lantern in one hand and a whiskey bottle in the other, and from the swaying manner in which he attempted to remain upright, it was obvious that he was thoroughly drunk.

"Evenin' Wes. Got here just in time for a little drink. Done cleaned the boys out at poker."

"I'm not here to drink or play cards, Jake," Dobler said as he stepped around the rear of his horse. "I came to pick up that stock and get some answers. Ward and the others are taking those beeves home right now, so all I've got left to do is get those answers. Where the hell is she?"

"Where's who?" Slater asked, lurching to one side while aiming the bottle at his lips.

Dobler was on the porch in one bound, and he knocked the whiskey bottle to one side with a vicious slap of his palm. The bottle clunked against the wall and then rolled down the slanting porch.

"You know who the hell I'm talking about, damn you! Have you got the girl or not?"

"The girl?" Slater asked, blinking his eyes and watching the bottle roll away in the darkness before adjusting his blurred vision on Dobler once more. "You mean Lee Ellen?"

"What ever in hell her name is. Dugan's daughter. Have you got her?"

Slater glanced away and cleared his throat nervously. "Well, ah . . . not exactly."

"What do you mean, 'not exactly,' you filthy goddamned drunk! Either she's here or she isn't, now which is it?"

"She was here, but she ain't right now, Wes. She kinda . . . kinda . . . got took away from us." Then Slater pasted a hopeful grin on his face as he continued, "But we're gonna get her back, Wes. We got a plan, me an' ol' Reeves. We'll get her back."

Exasperation was evident on Dobler's face as he stared up at the huge man looming over him, and there was something slightly comic about the outraged smaller man holding one so large at bay. "Well, where the hell is she?" he demanded, his patience nearly gone.

"You ain't gonna like it, Wes," Slater said tentatively.

"I don't like it already, dammit!"

"You're gonna like it less."

"I couldn't like it less, damn you. Now I'm going to ask you once more, real slow and easy, and I expect an answer. Where the hell is she?"

Slater watched him as if expecting a blow, before glancing away. "At the army post, Wes. The army's got her."

"What!"

"See?" Slater replied cautiously. "I told you you could like it less."

"Well Jesus-jumped-up-Christ! What the hell's she doing at a goddamned army post?"

"Gettin' over a gunshot wound."

91

Dobler's lips moved as if to speak, but no words came forth. Dumbfounded, he looked away. There were two primary goals in his mind at that moment, the first of which was to resist the overwhelming urge to kill Slater on the spot. The second was to contain the scream of rage and frustration building in his throat. Finally, after a long silence, he looked back at Slater.

"There is more, I imagine?" he asked.

"Yeah, Wes. There's more. Lots more."

"I was afraid of that," Dobler replied with a weary sigh. "Is there any whiskey left in that pigsty behind you?"

Slater's eyes brightened, and the look of certain doom melted from his face. "Lotsa whiskey, Wes. I made sure of that for ya," he replied, turning toward the door with a welcoming gesture of his hand.

"I'm sure you did, for me, of course. I want to hear the rest of it, and for that dubious pleasure I'm definitely going to need a drink. Several drinks, I'm afraid," Dobler said flatly as he stepped inside. "You talk, I'll pour."

Dobler listened patiently with a glower on his face and drinking steadily in silence as Slater told him about the fight with the army patrol, how Lee Ellen had been shot and taken captive, about Reeves's visit to the post, and how the cattle had been recovered and taken to the brakes and put in with the others already there. When Slater had told all he could recall, Dobler filled his cup once more, then shoved the bottle toward the center of the table.

"Where did you find her, this Lee Ellen, or whatever her name is?"

"Same little jerkwater town where her pappy, old Dugan, lived. I got her to come with me by tellin' her he was still alive and that I knew where to find him."

"Does she still believe that?"

"Don't know for sure. Maybe. She tried to get away a couple of times, but I always found her and brought her back."

Dobler eyed the big man critically. "If she tried to get away, then what in hell was she doing on that raid?"

"Bixby was supposed to keep an eye on her, Wes," Slater replied weakly. "I . . . I had some other things—"

"You were drunk and passed out, or you never would have let her out of your sight, Slater," Dobler said with absolute conviction. "I know you too damned well to believe anything else."

"Well, I was a little tired and mighta had one drink too many. But—"

"*But*, your ass! You were drunk, just like you were tonight when I got here. Now look, dammit," Dobler continued, his eyes becoming hard, "I've got too much riding on this, I've come too far, and I'm too damned close to lose it all because of your drunkenness. You told me that Dugan gave her his portion of the map while you two were in prison. Did she have it?"

"No. He gave it to her, all right, but she said she memorized it and then burned the paper like her pa told her to. Dugan didn't tell me about that, Wes, I promise."

Dobler turned the tin cup with his fingertips in contemplation. "No, I suppose he didn't. He didn't trust us any more than the two of you did me. I can understand that, and I never held it against you. Once you were caught and sent to prison, I sat back and waited. You told me just about where you were when you and Dugan split up, and that he went one way with the money and you went the other. So I bought that damned ranch hoping it was buried on my ground, then the government went and put in that goddamned reservation. So, we aren't going to be able to just find it. We'll have to go straight to it. And the only way we can do that is to force Dugan's daughter to tell us what she knows." Dobler glanced up and said in conclusion, "Maybe you shouldn't have killed the old bastard after all."

"Maybe not," Slater agreed, sobering rapidly but licking his lips every time he glanced at the bottle just out of reach. "But we had talked about a two-way split, Wes, and when Dugan told me he'd given his part of the map to his daughter, it pissed me off so bad I cut his throat right on the spot. Since we needed her, we didn't need him anymore. How 'bout a drink, huh? Throat's kinda dry."

"Go ahead, there's not much else you can botch up tonight anyway. I think we've just about got those Sioux pushed far enough to where they'll make their move any day now. They came onto my ground hunting buffalo today, so they've got to be getting a little hungry. My boys killed two of them."

"That should get things stirred up pretty good," Slater replied, sloshing whiskey into a cup and draining it in a single gulp. "Now all we gotta do is get Lee Ellen back."

Noticing the tone in which Slater mentioned the girl's name,

Dobler looked up with mild curiosity. "Kind of sweet on her, are you, Jake?"

"Naw. Turn 'em upside down and they all look the same," Slater said with a nervous grin. "You know me."

"Yes, I do. That's what worries me. Don't let that get in the way of our reason for being here, and don't get too damned sweet on her until this thing is over." Dobler watched his companion closely, looking for any adverse reaction as he added, "You just might have to do a little knife work on her to get her to talk. Wouldn't be an easy thing to do to a girl friend."

Whiskey spilled over the side of Slater's cup as he looked up sharply from his pouring. "It won't come to that, Wes. She'll talk. I know she will."

"She'd better. You mentioned a plan to get her out of that army post. Let's hear it, and it better be damned good."

"It is, Wes. It is. I came up with it myself," Slater replied. Hitching his chair closer to the table and leaning forward eagerly, he began detailing the plan. "There's this photographer, ya see, and—"

seven _____

"Where do you think he is, Windy?" Kincaid asked as they stopped their horses in the yard before the agency, and watched the darkened building, which was now bathed in soft moonlight. "It's damned near nine o'clock. You'd think he'd be here by now if he was going to be."

"Yup, you'd think so," Windy replied, instinctively searching the dark shadows as he spoke. "Old Roy ain't much given to a love of horses in the first place, and he sure as hell ain't fond of ridin' after nightfall. Don't look like there's been any kind of ruckus, so I imagine he's all right."

"Let's hope so, anyway. There's no sense in us tryin' to find him in the dark, so we might as well go in and make some coffee and wait for him here."

"He's usually got a bottle hid around the cupboard someplace, Matt," Windy replied as he swung down. "That sounds a mite more appealin' to me than coffee."

"I'm all for that. Corporal," Kincaid said, stepping from his saddle, "post a guard, then have the men make themselves as comfortable as possible. We'll be staying here until the agent gets back."

"Certainly, sir. What's the password?"

"Stearns. Roy Stearns."

"Yes, sir."

Kincaid followed the scout into the agency, dug out a match, and lit two lamps while Windy rummaged through the cupboards until he found a half-filled bottle of whiskey. Retrieving two coffee cups from the counter, he slid them onto the table, pulled the cork free with his teeth, and poured generously while pushing a chair back with his boot.

"Here's to old Roy," Windy said, hoisting his cup as he sank onto the seat. Then he added, just before the cup touched his lips, "Wherever in hell he is."

Kincaid matched the toast, drank, and then propped a boot on the corner of a chair. "I've been thinking about those holes you said you saw, Windy, and that old Reb who claims to have dug them. Didn't you say the other day that they never recovered the money taken in that last robbery by Dugan and Slater?"

"That's what they say. Supposed to be in the neighborhood of fifty thousand dollars."

"I thought so. Doesn't it seem a bit coincidental that Slater shows up now with Dugan's daughter?"

"Not at all. If they hid their loot around here somewheres, they'd sure as hell come back lookin' for it after they got out of prison."

Kincaid nodded. "Yes, I thought about that. But why his daughter? Why not Dugan himself?"

"Old Dugan might have caught himself a severe case of lead poisoning. Seems to be a disease fatal to most bank robbers."

"All right, but then where does Dobler fit in? He's the one who hired a man to dig, and the holes are on his property and adjacent to the reservation. Could it be that he got wind of the fact that some stolen money might be hidden on his ground, and he's trying to find it before the men who buried it do?"

"Could be," Windy allowed, reaching for the bottle again. "That'd be plenty of reason to try and keep the Sioux away, and that kind of money in exchange for a couple of lives just might be a proper trade to him."

"Gus said that the leader of those rustlers mentioned working for the Flying M spread, and he was pushing cattle with that brand. Maybe Slater went to work for Dobler to get close to where the cache is. Come to think of it, Brock didn't mention *who* was paying him to dig."

Kincaid paused to recall, then said, "No, wait a minute, He said that he worked for Dobler and that his job was to dig. He was specific about that. So Dobler, not Slater, at least directly, is the one searching for something."

"Came right back to your tail again, huh, Matt?" Windy asked with a grin. "Somebody is lookin' for somethin'. The girl mentioned Slater's name in connection with stolen government cattle, a dead thief worked for Dobler, and Dobler is diggin' holes in the ground when he's not shootin' at the Sioux. A lot to go on, but nowhere to go."

"Morris said that the girl told him she was afraid for her life, and that if she testified against Slater, he would kill her or have her killed. So she—"

"Halt! Who goes there!"

Both Kincaid and Mandalian heard the guard's challenge, and rising in unison, they moved toward the door.

"What the hell do you mean, 'who goes there'?" came a grumbling reply. "I go there, that's who the hell goes there!"

"Halt, or I'll fire! Corporal!"

"What the hell is this and who the hell are you?" asked an angry and throughly impatient voice from somewhere in the darkness. "I live here and work here, goddammit!"

"What's the password?"

"Password? Oh, shit! Look, soldier, I don't know what in Christ's name you think you're up to, but my name is Roy Stearns, by God, and I'm comin' through! Now put that gun down and get the hell out of my way!"

"It's all right, soldier!" Kincaid called from the center of the yard. "Let him pass!"

"Matt? Is that you?" Stearns asked, riding past the guard and urging an ancient horse forward with repeated flailings of his heels. "You're just the man I'm looking for."

"And I'm just the man you found, Roy," Kincaid replied as the elderly agent passed from the shadows and into the moonlight, then lowered himself from the saddle with some difficulty. "Should be a drink or two of your whiskey left in the house."

"Don't worry about it, Matt," Stearns said with a smile, as he shook both men's hands and clapped Windy on the shoulder. "I've got plenty more. Damn, am I glad to see you two. I was just on my way to Number Nine to find you. We've got problems, bad problems."

Kincaid signaled to a soldier standing by and said, "Put this horse up for old Roy here, and make sure its got feed and water."

"Yes, sir."

"Shoot the son of a bitch, for all I care," Stearns growled over his shoulder as he stomped into the building. "Damnedest way to get around ever conceived by the mind of man. Come on in and let's have a drink. I could sure as hell use one."

Kincaid and Mandalian followed the little agent inside and waited while he found a third cup, poured drinks all around, then plopped onto a chair after rubbing his buttocks in obvious pleasure.

"Now that's more like it. Seats weren't made to move, and especially not up and down. That old sonofabitch is going to be the death of me." Then he added as an afterthought, "If the Sioux don't take care of that little chore first."

"How do you mean that, Roy?" Kincaid asked. "Windy here thinks a couple of warriors might have been shot today. Have you heard anything?"

Stearns adjusted his wire-rimmed glasses, took a drink, and folded his fingers over an ample paunch as he leaned back in the chair.

"Heard anything!" he scoffed with a high-pitched, rather humorless chuckle. "Hell, Matt. I heard it all. That's where I just came from, the reservation. I saw what was supposed to have been a war party go by here late this afternoon, with two braves facedown and a third one being supported by two others. I went over to find out what happened and see if I could help."

"Two dead, Roy?" Windy asked somberly.

"Yup. Two blown all to hell."

"And the third?"

"He isn't dead, but he damned sure will be within twenty-four hours."

"How badly was he shot?" Kincaid inquired.

The old agent shook his head and waved a dismissing hand.

"He wasn't. But he might as well have been, if he dies. Beaver Claw is raising hell over there about the white men putting a curse on the boy, and he's determined to see some scalps lifted in retaliation."

Confused, Kincaid looked first at Windy before glancing again at the agent. "What do you mean, Roy? You seem to have left a little something out."

"Sorry, Matt. Sorry," Stearns replied, taking another drink then wiping his mouth on a sleeve. "Guess the old mind's a little befuddled with all this shit going on. Ever been around a hospital, Matt?"

"No, can't say that I have. Why?"

"Well, I was once, when my wife died. Anyway, they brought a young feller in whose symptoms were just like that warrior's. Severe stomach pain just in front and to the left of the right hip. Dizziness, nausea, a high fever. He hadn't been shot either, but he died anyway." The agent squinted and watched Kincaid closely. "His appendix had burst before they could operate on him."

"Appendix? Do you mean this warrior has appendicitis?"

"That's what I mean. I'm not absolutely positive, but I'd lay fair odds that that's what it is. And what's worse, if he dies because of some damned 'white man's curse,' our problems have only just begun. I suppose you'd like to know who it is?"

"The question had crossed my mind, Roy," Kincaid replied with a tight smile.

"Striking Hawk. The only son of Kills Many Bear, who has been, up till now at least, the only sensible person in that whole damned tribe. If it weren't for him, Beaver Claw would have led those people off that reservation two months ago, and he certainly will now. His nephew was one of the two braves that got killed. He's not in a mood to listen, and he will be going after scalps once the burial ceremonies are over."

"Damn," Kincaid said softly. "And you think Striking Hawk will die as well?"

"I'm sure of it, if he's got what I think he has. The only treatment he's getting now is a bunch of medicine men dancing around him, shaking gourds full of beads and chanting to those gods of theirs."

"What would the proper treatment be?"

"An operation. I was curious when that young feller I men-

99

tioned earlier died, so I asked a couple of doctors around the hospital about it. They said the operation wasn't all that difficult, but timing was critical, with damned little room for delay." Stearns rubbed the stubble along his jaw in contemplation before offering a hopeless shrug. "There isn't a doctor within a hundred miles of here that I'd trust to do the job if it were me, let alone risk having a Sioux chief's son die under a white man's knife."

"But you already said we'll be held responsible anyway, because of that curse business Beaver Claw is spreading around," Kincaid insisted. "So, by trying to save the boy's life, we won't be any worse off than we are already, no matter how he dies—*if* he does."

"I suppose that's true, but there's not much point in speculating on the subject. Like I said, there isn't a doctor within one hundred miles who—"

"Yes, there is, Roy. And I can have him here by sunup, or damned close."

The old agent arched an eyebrow quizzically. "If you're thinking about Doc Barkley, Matt, then you've got to be out of your goddamned mind. I wouldn't let him operate on that old horse of mine, much as I hate the son of a bitch, let alone Kills Many Bear's son."

"I don't mean Barkley. I mean a first-class surgeon—an army doctor named Frederick Morris. I've seen him work, and he damned well knows what he's doing."

"And where in God's name do you expect to find him?"

"At Number Nine. He showed up a few days back. I'll explain it all later, there isn't time to waste now," Kincaid said, speaking quickly and turning toward Windy. "What do you think, Windy? Is it worth a try?"

"Could be, Matt. Then again, it could be a waste of time—or worse."

"Or worse?"

"Could be. All Indians are very touchy about their medicine, and the Sioux are the worst of the lot. They believe in the healing ways of their medicine men, and tryin' to convince the Sioux that the white man's medicine is stronger could be a real chore. Whoever tries it sure as hell won't be real popular. That's the waste-of-time part. The worse part might be in the proof."

"How, Windy?" Stearns asked.

"If we bring a white doctor in here and he cures a boy that would have died otherwise, we'd be makin' fools out of the medicine men, and Beaver Claw in particular. He's powerful, he's already got a burr under his blanket, and he might turn mean just to save face, if nothin' else."

"Whose decision would that be, according to tribal custom, Windy?" Kincaid asked.

"Kills Many Bear's. He might be willin' to listen to us just to save his boy, but if he does and the kid lives, we might have a medicine war on our hands along with everything else. And that's the worst kind, Matt. You're just as aware of that as I am."

"Which would play into the hands of whoever is stirring all this up in the first place," Matt replied, propping an elbow on his knee and resting his chin on the heel of his hand. "So we're stuck either way. If Striking Hawk dies, it's because of a white man's curse. If he lives as the result of a white doctor's training and skill, we make fools out of the medicine men and risk a war. But I don't think we would be risking all that much, since war, or at least a retaliatory raid led by Beaver Claw, seems inevitable. I'd rather risk seeing him lose face than do nothing and let Kills Many Bear's son die when we might have prevented it."

"Then that's your decision, Matt?" Stearns asked. "To get that doctor of yours out here and have him operate?"

"Yes, it is. Kills Many Bears has tried his best to live up to the conditions of the treaty. To let his son die would be an unplanned victory for whoever is behind all this. If I can prevent it, I don't intend to see Kills Many Bear have to pay that kind of price for something that's none of his doing in the first place. I'll take whatever responsibility goes with that decision."

Windy nodded. "I'm with you all the way, Matt. Want me to talk with the chief?"

"Yes, we'll both go." Kincaid turned to Stearns. "Can we use your agency here for an operating room, Roy?"

"You bet. I'm with you one hundred percent. I'll have things set up by the time you're ready, if the chief goes along with it."

"There's quite a bit of risk involved, Roy," Kincaid cautioned. "If the boy dies during the operation, we will be held directly responsible."

"To hell with a bunch of risk, Matt. Just bein' here is risk, and I'm too old to really give much of a shit one way or the other. Let's save that boy's life if we can."

"Good," Kincaid replied, rising and stepping toward the door. "Thanks, Roy. I'll send Corporal Wojensky and some of the squad back to the post right now. They should return with the doctor by sunup. In the meantime, Windy and I will go over to the reservation and talk with Kills Many Bear."

The agent studied the lieutenant over the rim of his cup as he downed the last of the whiskey. "Be careful, Matt. You too, Windy. They were in a real fighting mood when I was over there earlier."

The scout smiled as he rose to follow Kincaid. "Never seen a Sioux that wasn't, Roy. We'll be back by dawn."

"Corporal!" Kincaid yelled as he stepped outside and went down the steps.

"Yes, sir?" Wojensky replied, materializing from the darkness.

"Take two men with you and ride back to the post tonight. Leave the others here to protect the agency. Bring Lieutenant Morris back and be here by sunrise—sooner, if possible—and tell Captain Conway that two Sioux warriors have been killed and a third is suffering from what we believe to be appendicitis. Tell him it is the son of Kills Many Bear, and that he will surely die if not given proper medical treatment. Also, tell him we're about one day away from a war here, and I suggest sending an additional squad back with you, just in case the Sioux seek revenge as we think they will. Be sure and have the lieutenant bring all his surgical equipment. Have you got that?"

"Yes, sir. We'll be back as quickly as we can, Lieutenant."

"Good. Windy and I are going over to the Sioux village tonight. If we aren't back by the time you get here, assume we have been killed or taken captive, and initiate proper procedures."

"Yes, sir," the corporal said, returning Kincaid's hasty salute, then watching the officer swing onto his horse's back, Mandalian doing likewise. Immediately the two of them were gone, and Wojensky began barking out instructions to his men.

"You know Kills Many Bear personally, don't you, Windy?" Kincaid asked as they galloped their horses side by side across the darkened plains. "Better than I do, I mean. I've only met the man a time or two, and that was under pretty formal circumstances."

"Yeah, I know him 'bout as well as any white man could," Mandalian replied. "We've fought against each other in war and smoked together in peace. He's a fair and honest man, as far as I know. If we come to him in peace, he'll talk with us. He may not listen, but he will let us talk."

"That's all we can ask for, under the circumstances. How about Beaver Claw?"

"He's a horse of a different color, Matt. Being a powerful medicine chief like he is, he's very moody and suspicious of white men. He doesn't make a big secret of the fact that he would like to be in Kills Many Bear's position, and I wouldn't be surprised to see him use any situation that might give him an advantage. They were great friends years ago, but that friendship has kinda gone to hell lately. Deep inside, I don't think he's all that bad. He just don't understand that times have changed. If we do save that lad's life, he ain't gonna like it one damned bit. It'll cost him a lot of face, and it might cause him to challenge for leadership outright. The Sioux will be split down the middle, and we'll have that medicine war on our hands that I was talkin' about."

"From a personal point of view, it sounds like he would have more to gain by having Striking Hawk die than live," Kincaid replied, slowing his mount to negotiate a dry wash. "If he dies, that's just the way the gods wanted it. But if he lives, then the white man's curse that he's been talking about will be just so much hogwash."

"Yup. Beaver Claw is no fool. Unless he knew the boy was sick enough to die, he wouldn't have put himself out on a limb like that. The Indians are big on predictions, and it means strong medicine to get one right. Yeah, he knows Striking Hawk is gonna die—one way or another."

Kincaid allowed a tight grin as he glanced across at his chief scout. "Beaver Claw might have gotten lucky on some other guesses, but not this one. He hasn't met Dr. Frederick Morris yet."

It was nearly midnight when they stopped their horses on a prominent swell and gazed at the red glow illuminating the prairie possibly a mile away. The flames from an exceptionally large fire licked at the blackness in a dancing, almost caressing

103

shimmer, and the sound of chanting could be heard, carried on the stillness by a lilting westerly breeze.

"That'd be the death fire, Matt," Mandalian said, bobbing the barrel of his Sharps toward the blaze. "They'll sing and dance around that all night long, workin' themselves into a frenzy by dawn. It means a chief or the son of a chief has died, or is just about ready to cash in. They're calling on the spirits of other warriors killed in battle to guide his spirit to the Other Place, as they call it."

"And if he does die?"

"Then they go on the warpath against whoever did it." Windy spat to one side and added, "Which means us and that mighty fine curse of ours. We'd better walk our horses on in from here. They'll have us surrounded any minute, anyway."

Kincaid urged his horse forward in stride with Mandalian's, and as if the scout had somehow felt their presence, a band of mounted warriors closed about them before they had traveled fifty yards. The scout raised his hand shoulder-high, palm turned forward. A fierce-looking warrior blocked their path with his pony and gave no acknowledgment of the peace sign offered by Windy, choosing instead to keep both hands firmly gripped on the Spencer he held waist-high, aimed at Kincaid.

"I come in peace to see my old friend, Kills Many Bear," Windy said evenly. "This here is a powerful white chief from Washington. His name is Lieutenant Kincaid and he wants to smoke in peace with your great chief. Tell one of your braves to take that message to Kills Many Bear. Tell him my name is Windy Mandalian, but he knows me a tad better as the Snake."

The Indian continued to stare at them impassively for long moments before turning to another brave and speaking rapidly in their native tongue. Then the warrior wheeled his mount and rode away at a dead run, while his companions waited where they were with weapons trained on the two white men.

"I would've made you a general, Matt," Windy said with an easy grin as they sat there, "but Kills Many Bear knows better. That other asshole wouldn't know a general from a buck-assed private."

"Thanks just the same, Windy. They are very impressed with titles, aren't they?"

"Yup. You could be the dumbest son of a bitch who ever wore a pair of boots, and that couldn't matter less to them as long as you're Chief So-and-So."

"Reminds me of some generals I've known."

Windy chuckled, bit off a chew of tobacco, and leaned back to wait for the warrior's return.

He was back in less than five minutes, and nodded curtly at Windy before jerking his pony around and leading the way toward the village. The cacophony of chants had suddenly died, and they were surrounded by an eerie silence broken only by the sound of hooves swishing through the tall grass and the soft murmur of crickets singing in the distance.

As they entered the circle of light, the warriors split off in either direction, and Kills Many Bear looked up at them from where he was seated by the fire. Beaver Claw stepped from a tipi immediately to the rear, and stood beside Kills Many Bear with his arms folded across his chest, staring sullenly at the two white men. On a cue from Windy, Kincaid swung down and they stepped forward to face the chief.

"How are you, my old friend?" the scout said with great sincerity as Kills Many Bear rose to greet them. "We come in peace and with a heavy heart for your sadness."

The chief nodded, and his eyes showed some affection for the tall scout dressed in fringed leather. "You are welcome in my village," he said simply, with a glance at Kincaid.

"This is Lieutenant Matt Kincaid. He says he's had the honor of meeting you a time or two before, Chief."

Kills Many Bear nodded again. "The lieutenant has been fair and honest with me. He is welcome in peace," the chief said, making a sweeping gesture with his hand toward some blankets spread across the ground.

When the three of them were seated, Kills Many Bear took up a long stone pipe, with twin eagle feathers attached just beneath the bowl, which he offered first to Windy and then to Kincaid. After each had taken several puffs, the chief did likewise and laid the pipe aside.

"Why have you come to my village?"

"We have heard of the sickness of your son," Kincaid replied. "We have come to offer help and express our concern."

Kills Many Bear glanced at Beaver Claw impassively, then back at the two white men. "Our medicine chiefs have said he is dying from a white man's curse. If they cannot break the spell, he will die."

"I know of their power and great medicine," Kincaid continued in a tone of respect. "The gods smile down upon them."

"The will of the gods shall be obeyed."

"Yes, and that's as it should be. Do you think your son will die?"

"Yes," Kills Many Bear said with a slow, deep nod. "The medicine chiefs have said it shall be so."

"May I see him?" Kincaid asked.

"Why?"

Kincaid looked at Beaver Claw and spoke to both men at once. "Because if it is a white man's curse that's taking your son away from you, there might be something I know about it that your great medicine chiefs do not. I offer my help with all due respect to their wisdom."

"He will die," Beaver Claw said flatly.

"I see. Then it shouldn't hurt if I have a look," Kincaid replied. "If he is going to die, then there is no harm I can do him."

Kills Many Bear looked first at the medicine chief and then at Kincaid. "You know something of this curse?"

"Yes, I believe I do. And I know the cure."

Anger flashed in Beaver Claw's dark eyes. "There is no cure for the white man's curse. I know much of these things, and nothing can be done. The gods have told me of this, and they direct my hands."

"Do the gods wish to see a young warrior, son of a great chief, taken away with no scars to show for his battle with the enemy? No, I think not. If he is to fall, it can only be after he has fought bravely like his father. The Sioux will need a great chief to lead them through the troubled times ahead. A leader much like you, Kills Many Bear. I think it strange that the gods would choose to select his spirit to be taken to the Other Place when he has not yet proven his manhood."

Kincaid knew instinctively that he should say no more, and he held his silence while allowing the chief to think and formulate a response. Finally, Kills Many Bear shifted his gaze from Kincaid to Mandalian.

"What do you think of this, my old friend? The Snake has great wisdom; he would not have been victorious in battle so many times if this were not so. Speak, and I will know your words come from your heart."

Windy replied in a slow, emotionless voice, "My wisdom is no greater than yours. I say the lieutenant should see Striking Hawk. He has knowledge of white men's ways that neither of us have. If it is a white man's curse, then a white man should know the cure, I reckon."

"He will die!" Beaver Claw snarled, shaking the rattle in his hand furiously at the tipi opening behind him. "If a white man goes in and touches Striking Hawk, it will only make the curse that much stronger."

"How much worse can a curse be than one that kills you?" Windy asked laconically. "That's about as bad as they can get, I'd say."

"This is a trick, Kills Many Bear!" the medicine chief said, turning on his counterpart. "Your eyes are so blinded by the white man's promises that you believe them over the advice of a Sioux medicine chief. Beaver Claw has great medicine, and I have talked with the gods. Striking Hawk will die, and it is they who have caused his death. His spirit will be taken to the Other Place only if I guide it there. Do not let a white man touch him or the gods will be angry and even my great medicine will be too little. His spirit will wander forever."

Kills Many Bear had listened patiently to both arguments, and now he closed his eyes briefly before opening them again and looking at Kincaid.

"You can see my son," he said softly. "I am more concerned with the words of one who says he can prevent his death than the words of one who only wishes to guide his spirit away. Come," he concluded, rising and moving toward the opening. "I will show him to you."

"Thank you for your confidence in me," Kincaid said as he stood, brushed past an unyielding Beaver Claw, and followed the chief to duck inside the tipi.

Striking Hawk was lying stretched out on a thick bed of pelts, and the shadows cast by a single torch flickered across his drawn face. His long black hair was damp with sweat, and his upper torso glistened in the weak light. Even though his obvious intention was to show no outward sign of emotion, his teeth were gritted tightly against the pain, and clouded, yellowish eyes stared vacantly at the poles lashed together above his head. The close air of the tipi was rich with the smell of herbs simmering over a tiny fire and the odor of various ointments that had been applied to his body.

Kills Many Bear stood back silently and watched Kincaid kneel beside his son to pull the robe away and gently probe the swollen area over the right hip. Striking Hawk flinched involuntarily and his Adam's apple bobbed with a sharp, breath-catching swallow.

"I'm sorry, Striking Hawk," Kincaid said, without taking

his eyes off the young warrior's lower abdomen. "I'll be as gentle as I can be."

As he worked, Kincaid tried to remember the description Stearns had given of the symptoms associated with appendicitis. After nearly five minutes, he covered Striking Hawk's stomach again with the robe and turned toward Kills Many Bear.

"There is no question that your son is seriously ill and might die no matter what we do. But he is not suffering from a white man's curse. He is suffering from a thing we call appendicitis, and it can be fatal if not properly treated." He motioned toward the cauldron with one hand. "With no disrespect for Beaver Claw or the medicines your people believe in, that is not the proper treatment."

Kills Many Bear nodded, and his gaze drifted to his son's face. "What is the proper treatment?"

"An operation to remove the infected appendix. I am not a doctor, and surgery would be required."

"Surgery?" the chief asked, defensively curious. "I do not know this word."

"In this case, it means that a small incision must be made, a small cut with a sharp knife. The appendix is removed and the opening stitched together once more. There is a doctor at our post right now who can do this thing. I cannot promise you that your son will live if the operation is performed, but I can promise you that he will certainly die if it is not. I have sent some of my men to get the doctor and bring him to the agency to do what we can to save your son's life. He will be there when the sun rises in the morning."

Kills Many Bear watched Kincaid with mild curiosity. "Why would you do this for my son?"

"Because he deserves to live. You have been a fair and honest man with us. We have taken much away from you, and there's nothing I can do about that. But if we can give you back your son's life, then we can at least repay you in part for your losses. We want to live in peace with you, and we want to live in peace with your son as well, when he is the chief of the Sioux. A great Sioux chief never forgets a kindness. Your son will be no different."

Kills Many Bear looked once at his son, and then his somber gaze turned to Kincaid.

"Your doctor will do what you have said to my son. But

it will be done here and nowhere else. Your doctor will stay here until I know if my son will live or die. If he lives, your doctor can go free. If he dies, your doctor will die in a similar manner. Is that agreed?"

Kincaid shook his head. "I haven't got the power to place another man's life in jeopardy without his consent. That's a decision only he can make."

"Then you have no faith in this doctor of yours, or his medicine, but you ask me to give my son's life to him?"

"I have more than faith; I have absolute confidence." Kincaid watched the chief and held his words momentarily for greater impact. "I will take his place and be your prisoner to kill however you wish. If Striking Hawk lives, you will keep your people on the reservation and not take up the warpath in retaliation for the deaths of your two warriors. I will find the guilty ones and bring them to justice."

"That is agreed," Kills Many Bear said with his customary slow nod. "My son's life for yours. If he dies, you die."

Kincaid stepped from the tent and stopped beside Windy Mandalian, who grinned at him slyly.

"Your fat's pretty much in the fire, Matt, if Morris has a bad day tomorrow. You know that."

"I know it," Kincaid replied, swinging onto his saddle and turning his horse away. "And it's not real comforting to know that this will be only his second operation. Come on. Let's get back to the agency."

Neither of them noticed the look of hatred and outrage on Beaver Claw's face, nor did they see him spin on his heel and stride toward the section of the village where the braves loyal to him had silently gathered.

eight ————————————————

Even though he felt exhausted, emotionally drained, Lieutenant Morris was having a difficult time falling asleep as he lay on his cot with his hands behind his head, staring upward at the blankness of a darkened ceiling. He tried to dismiss the tension he felt as a normal reaction associated with the swirl of events that had gone on about him since his arrival at Outpost Number Nine. He had certainly found himself in a unique situation and one that would be unsettling to anyone expecting an entirely different set of circumstances within which to begin a career in medicine. But he knew what was disturbing him, and he could feel her presence, even though their beds were separated by a distance of ten feet.

The rise and fall of her shallow, relaxed breathing; the smell of her body freshly bathed and perfumed; the shaft of moonlight touching the corner of her pillow and revealing her smooth cheek outlined against auburn hair: It was a combination of these things that disturbed Dr. Morris's mind, and they made him feel both ashamed and elated at the same time. From a professional point of view, he knew his feelings toward her were totally wrong and in conflict with his determination to maintain a respectable distance between patient and physician. But his feelings toward her went beyond his ability to be totally objective in his attitude and concern for her welfare.

True, she was the first patient he had ever saved from death, or even treated, as a matter of fact. He had long since admitted, however, that that was but a small part of his strong attraction to her. She was so beautiful, so soft and vulnerable; almost like a full-grown adult who had somehow reverted back to infancy. And then there was the way she watched him as he moved about the small room in the performance of his duties. It was as if her eyes never left him, and even though she hadn't spoken since the day she had seen that drifter, she seemed to be in constant communication with him and almost pleading to be understood and cared for. And when he would turn unexpectedly and catch her eyes upon him, she would glance quickly away and a pink tinge would creep into her cheeks. In those moments he would experience an almost uncontrollable desire to reach out and take her face in his hands and lower his lips to hers.

Seeking to think of anything but her, Morris shifted to an equally uncomfortable position on his hard cot and wondered what the time might be. He guessed it must be long after midnight, and he sighed wearily, wishing for sleep to sweep mercifully over him and take him away from his thoughts until the welcome light and distractions of another day would steal him from the haunting night-thoughts he was now experiencing. Finally, nearly half an hour later, he slipped into a fitful, dozing sleep. The gentle rapping of knuckles on the door jarred him to wakefulness once more.

"Yes?" he answered softly. "Who is it?"

"Corporal Wojensky, sir. Lieutenant Kincaid sent me."

"Just a moment, soldier," Morris replied, slipping out of bed and pulling a robe over his night clothes. "I'll be right out."

He opened the door a crack and looked out upon the moonlit parade. "Yes, Corporal? What is it? Please keep your voice down, I've got an extremely ill patient inside."

"Yes, sir. Sorry to disturb you like this, but Lieutenant Kincaid said it was urgent."

"Yes? Go on?"

"He sent me to get you and take you back to the agency with me. There's a man there who might have appendicitis, and he wants you to come immediately to treat him."

"Where?"

"The Sioux reservation, sir. It's about a four-hour ride from here. He told me to be back by dawn, and if we're going to make it, we'll have to leave immediately. He also told me to tell you to bring all your doctoring equipment."

Confused, Morris ran a hand through his hair and turned to look inside the room once more. He could see the woman watching him silently, and he felt a strange chill trickle down his spine.

"Well, I don't know," Morris said hesitantly. "That will take me away from my patient for an awfully long time. Can't the individual be brought here?"

"No, sir. The sick man is an Indian and he can't be brought here. He is the son of a chief, and he might die if you don't operate on him. Besides, sir, I was given a direct order by Lieutenant Kincaid to bring you back there. Pardon my saying so, sir, but I'll see that his order is carried out, come hell or high water."

Morris turned wearily toward the doorway.

"All right. I'll need a few minutes to collect my things. And I'll need a mount, of course."

"That's being taken care of already, sir. I have a message to convey to the captain, and then I'll be back for you. We should be gone in five minutes."

Across the parade Morris could see men running from lamplit barracks in the direction of the stables and he shook his head in disbelief at the strange breed of soldiers he had somehow come to be one of. Closing the door behind him, he pulled on his clothes and boots, then lit a lamp, which he hooded carefully to provide the least illumination while packing his medical bag. Once the task was completed, he took his hat from the rack, blew out the lamp, and hesitated by Lee Ellen's bed.

After a momentary search for words, he said softly, "Are you awake?"

The woman didn't reply, but he could tell by her breathing that she was awake. "I've been called away for a short while, but I shouldn't be gone too long. You're going to be all right. I'm sure Mrs. Conway and Mrs. Cohen will look in on you. Please don't move about too much, and take your medicine."

After trying to think of something more to say, he gave up, squeezed her hand gently, and took up his bag and moved toward the door. Just as his hand touched the latch, he heard a tentative voice from behind him in the darkness.

"Doctor?"

Morris turned quickly and moved back to the bed. "Yes, Miss Dugan?"

"Please, call me Lee Ellen."

"Thank you. I will. You'll be just fine. I'll be back as quickly as I can. I hate to go, Lee Ellen. Believe me, I hate to leave you," he said, gently taking up her hand once again. "But you won't be alone. There is a whole company of soldiers here to protect you."

"I know, but I... I'd rather have you."

Embarrassment flushed Morris's face, and he was glad for the darkness. "And I'd rather stay, but a man is sick, and I have to do what I can to help him, just like I have for you."

She looked up at him and she seemed so alone, so fragile. Almost like a beautiful plant that could not be exposed to strong sunlight. "Will you come and see me the minute you get back?"

"Yes, I will. The very minute I get back."

Again the rapping came at the door, and Morris started to turn away as Wojensky said, "Lieutenant? We have to leave now, sir."

"Coming, Corporal," Morris replied, lifting his hand from hers but stopping its motion when her fingers closed about it. "Don't be frightened, Lee Ellen," he said reassuringly. "Everything is going to be all right."

"I'm not frightened for myself, Doctor—I mean about living or dying. I'm frightened because I'm afraid I might lose you, that you might be hurt or killed."

"Nonsense, Lee Ellen. I'm just a doctor, even though I wear an army uniform. No one has any cause to hurt me."

"I'm still afraid," she said. "Would you do something for me before you go?"

"Or course. Anything. What is it?"

"Would you... would you... kiss me? I want to have something to remember you by if I never see you again."

Morris could feel the heat spreading across the back of his neck, and his throat felt tight and dry. "You will see me again, I promise you that. I would never let anything prevent my return. You're very...special to me, too." Then he leaned down quickly and kissed her lips. "I...I...better go now," he said in a husky voice as he pulled away. "They're waiting for me."

Morris stepped quickly outside and pulled the door securely closed behind him. "I'm ready, Corporal," he said, clearing his throat and hoping his constricted tone would not be noticed.

"That's good, sir, The captain sends his best wishes. We will be escorted by a full squad, and we'll be riding hard. We have less than four hours until daylight."

"Yes, I understand," Morris replied as the squad cantered up with two mounts on lead. When they passed through the gates, they were riding at a full gallop and he felt a surge of excitement such as he had never fully experienced before. And it had nothing to do with the prospect of the coming surgery, riding at the head of a column of armed men, the possibility of war, or the apparent urgency of the situation at hand. It had to do entirely with a frail woman lying in the moonlight and turning her lips up to him, and a human emotion that had been entirely overlooked in the Hippocratic Oath.

"Guess we'd better get a move on, huh, Windy?" Kincaid said, checking his pocket watch as he pushed his coffee cup to one side. "It's two o'clock now, and we should be able to intercept Wojensky's squad in a couple of hours. Since we're not going to do the operation here, we can save a lot of time by cutting across to the village a little further to the east."

"Yeah, no point in havin' the doc come all the way back here," Mandalian replied, stifling a yawn with the back of his hand. "Think I might've dozed off for a minute or two there."

Stearns shook his head and stared at the two men through bleary eyes. "I don't know how in the hell you do it. You've been in a goddamned saddle all day and most of the night, and now you're ready to go again. Christ, two hours of that shit'll do me for a month, and then I don't ever want to see a horse again."

"Things could be worse, Roy."

"How'n hell do you figure that?"

Kincaid grinned, rising from the table. "We might have been attached to the regular infantry. I'll send somebody back after this thing is over to let you know where we stand."

"I'd appreciate it. Oh, Matt?"

Kincaid turned in the doorway. "What's on your mind?"

"You were just shittin' me, weren't you?"

"About what?"

"About your putting your life on the line in exchange for Striking Hawk's."

"No, I wasn't."

"But why? That's *his* appendix that went to hell, not yours, so it's his problem. His and the doctor's. Why'd you do it?"

"Because that's the only way I could get Kills Many Bear to give his word that he would keep his people on the reservation and leave the killers for the army to deal with. I figure the chance of preventing a war is worth the risk, and if I can do that, I'll only have done what I get paid to do."

"Damned noble of him, ain't it, Roy?" Windy asked with a lazy smile. "'Sides, he's got a little streak of crazy in him that's gotta get a little sunlight once in a while."

"I've always prided myself on knowing the difference between crazy and stupid, Windy. It wouldn't take a genius to figure out which way the wind blows in this case. Let's just hope that doctor knows what he's doing, 'cause it's damned sure Kincaid there doesn't."

"That doctor's greener'n spring grass, Roy," Windy replied, draping his saddlebags over his shoulder. "And old Matt here knows it. Maybe you do know the difference 'tween crazy and stupid, after all."

"Damned right I do," Stearns growled as the two men walked through the doorway. "But that doesn't mean I go around lookin' for a chance to prove it!"

Kincaid and Mandalian walked across the faintly illuminated yard toward their horses, and Windy said offhandedly, "You know, Matt, I think old Roy's a little concerned about you."

"And you're not?" Kincaid asked, stopping beside his mount and lifting a stirrup to tighten the cinch strap.

"Naw. Why should I be? That kid's appendix is so ripe it's gonna pop outta there like a melon seed from a little boy's mouth."

"You know something about it?"

"Not a helluva lot. More'n some, less'n others," Windy replied.

In accordance with a custom developed through years of riding together during the hours of darkness, neither man spoke and each reacted instinctively to the movements of the other, like two draft animals joined by a yoke. With their mounts separated by a distance of fifteen yards to make ambush less simple, they rode single file, alternating the lead approximately every hour due to the eyestrain of searching out the best possible trail. They kept to the sodded turf, avoiding rocky dry washes and hardpan to prevent the echo of hooves, which would signal their approach to an enemy lying in wait. It was the responsibility of the man in front to guide them, with his companion to the rear keeping an alert watch in all directions with weapons prepared to provide covering fire in the event that escape became necessary.

The pace of their mounts was regulated as well, and intended to cover the greatest amount of distance in the shortest period of time without jeopardizing the animals' safety to unseen objects or taxing their strength beyond the ability to maintain sustained flight over a considerable distance. They were both aware that a horse was a man's lifeline on the prairie.

As the lead changed for the second time, Mandalian said softly when Kincaid rode past him on his way to the front, "Two hours now, Matt. Must be near four o'clock."

"Yes, I know," Kincaid replied, also in a hushed tone, aware that the human voice had phenomenal carrying power on the flat plains. "We should be meeting the squad any minute now. At least we should pick up some sound."

Mandalian reined his horse in to fall back. "Yeah, we should. If they're on time. Hold it!" he said, more harshly this time. "Let's flatten an ear."

With that, the scout slid from his horse's back and pressed the side of his head against the prairie soil to listen intently for several moments before rising again. "That might be them. Sounds like eight, maybe ten horses."

"Good. We should cross their trail just up by that draw ahead. Let's go."

The seat of Windy's pants had no more than touched saddle leather when the first crashing explosion split the night silence. Several more weapons opened fire, and the angry red flame of muzzle flashes dotted the darkness, followed by the startled yells of men trying to control frightened mounts and return fire at the same time. Seconds later the blasting of rifles and revolvers could be heard from somewhere in the bottom of the

117

draw, but no muzzle flashes could be seen.

Mandalian's mount was beside Kincaid's instantly, and he jerked the plunging animal's head back with a sharp pull on the reins. "They've been jumped in the draw, Matt. You recognize any of the voices?"

"Yeah. I heard Wojensky telling his men to fall back and form a firing line. They were taken completely by surprise. It must have been by someone who knew they were going to the agency this morning."

"That leaves old Roy, Beaver Claw, and Kills Many Bear. Care to make a wager?"

"No, because we'll both be betting on the same man. Come on, let's get our boys out of this. You circle around and take them from the north flank, I'll close in on the south and wait until you fire before I make my move."

"Good a plan as any. Happy huntin'," Windy said with a grin as he drove his heels against his horse's flanks.

Kincaid listened to the rattling fire, which had lessened now as targets were picked by an opponent's muzzle flash, and he could easily detect that the attackers greatly outnumbered the defenders. He judged their number to be at least twenty or thirty, and he could hear at least six army Springfields returning fire. From the twin cross-draw holsters on his hips, he pulled his regulation Scofield and his distinctly non-army, mother-of-pearl-handled Colt. Holding his horse's reins along with the Scofield in his left hand, he heeled his mount slowly forward while waiting for Windy's first shot.

Thirty seconds later he heard the bellowing roar of Mandalian's Sharps, and saw a bright yellow hole open in the night and then close, followed by another. He sank the spurs home and his horse bolted forward at a dead run as he fired alternately with both pistols to give the impression of greater firepower. His mount was closing rapidly on the attackers, as was Mandalian's, and he could hear surprised exclamations in native Sioux as warriors quit their positions and ran toward horses held by handlers to the rear. Several weapons were turned in his direction, and he heard the sizzling snap of bullets through the air around him as he lowered his body across the horse's withers and continued to fire.

Kincaid could tell from the firing off to his right that Wojensky's squad was advancing toward the near side of the draw, and in the face of the combined firepower, the Sioux retreated en masse and their weapons went silent. Windy's Sharps continued to belch flame in the direction of fleeing targets, then he lowered his rifle and angled his horse toward Kincaid's.

"I'd say we timed that just about right, Matt," he offered as his horse cantered up. "We put a little shit in their britches."

"Yeah, I think so," Kincaid replied while loading fresh cartridges into the cylinder of his Scoff. "Think they've had enough?"

"I reckon so. Their only advantage, with light as bad as this, was surprise, and they ain't got that no more."

"That's pretty much the way I see it as well. Let's go down and check for casualties. It'll be light soon. We'll wait here until then and see what kind of damage we did to the Sioux."

The first man they met in the bottom of the draw was Wojensky, who said, "I'm sorry, Lieutenant. They took us by surprise. We were moving too fast to have point guards out, and they wouldn't have done any good in the dark, anyway. It's my fault, sir. I led my men into a trap."

"You did as you were instructed, Corporal. I told you to be back to the agency by dawn, and that was a tall order under any conditions. How many men did you lose, dead or wounded?"

"I don't know exactly, sir. I saw two go down with that first volley. One of 'em was ridin' right beside me. It was the doctor, sir. He was the first one hit."

"Lieutenant Morris?" Kincaid asked sharply.

"Yes, sir. He was there one second and gone the next."

"Well, of all the goddamned rotten luck," Kincaid said bitterly. "Was he killed?"

"Don't know, sir. Haven't had a chance to find him yet."

"No, of course you haven't. You did a good job in defending your position, Corporal. Now post some guards, and Windy and I'll find out what our casualty situation is. If we can, we'll be moving out after dawn."

"Yes, sir," Wojensky replied, moving away quickly and apparently mindless of the flesh wound across his thigh that caused a noticeable limp.

"Did you hear that, Windy?" Kincaid asked. "About Morris, I mean?"

"Yup. Damned shame to lose our ace in the hole."

"Just because he's missing doesn't mean he's dead, my friend. And I don't give a damn who he is or what he means to us, he's no more important to me than any of my other men. Let's spread out and check for dead and wounded."

When the sun touched the horizon and spread its reddish glow across the plains, three wounded soldiers were seated on the bank of the draw with fresh white bandages strapped over their injuries, but Dr. Morris was not among them. Kincaid patted the last man on the shoulder, rose to check the positioning of his sentries on the surrounding knolls, then turned to Wojensky.

"Any sign of Windy?"

"No, sir. His horse is over there, so he couldn't have gone far."

"I see," Kincaid said, glancing at the tall roan. "How about the doctor? Nothing either?"

"Nothing, sir. Think the Indians got him?"

"No, they wouldn't have had time."

"I guess not, the way you and Windy came chargin' up to the fight. Thanks, Lieutenant. It could have been a damned bloody mess if you hadn't showed up when you did."

"No thanks needed, Corporal. Check the draw once more, then—"

"Hey, Matt. Over here! I found him."

"That's Windy. Keep an eye on things here until I get back," Kincaid said, moving away as he spoke.

"Yes, sir."

Kincaid ran toward the sound of Windy's voice, and as he crested a small swell he saw the scout kneeling over a prone figure. His heart sank. "How bad is he, Windy?" he asked as he slowed to a reluctant walk. "Dead?"

"Nope, but he has been shot. Must have crawled over here and passed out during the fight. Haven't had a good look-see at him yet, but he's still breathin'," Mandalian replied, rolling the lieutenant over onto his back.

Blood had trickled into Morris's right eye from a gash across his forehead, and his right arm, encased in a bloody coat sleeve, lay limply across his stomach. By the time Kincaid had knelt down beside him, the scout's knife was out. He artfully cut the material away, then quickly examined the wound while speaking over his shoulder.

"He's been shot through the right forearm, Matt. Looks like its broken, but the bleedin' ain't too bad. 'Less'n he took a bullet somewhere that I can't see, he should be as good as a gold watch in a month or so."

120

"How about that wound across his forehead?"

"Hardly a scratch. Must've hit his head when he fell off his horse. He'll come around any minute now."

"Damn," Kincaid said under his breath as he sat back on his haunches. "This was all we needed."

Mandalian turned to look at Kincaid and said quietly, "He won't be doin' any cuttin' with that paw for quite a while, Matt." The scout paused, studying his friend. "Was he right-handed or left-handed?"

"Right-handed, Windy," Kincaid replied softly. "I remember that distinctly."

Mandalian nodded and turned to look at the rising sun. "It's half an hour past sunrise now, Matt. Whatcha gonna do?"

Kincaid stared at the doctor in silence, then rose and turned toward the crest of the swell. "Get some bandages and patch him up," he said as he strode away. "Just because he can't operate, that doesn't mean he can't tell someone else how to."

nine _____

"Afternoon, friend."

At the sound of the flat, less-than-cordial voice behind him, the man with his head beneath the black cloth struggled to free himself of the material clinging to his shoulders. He had been so engrossed in setting up his shot that he hadn't heard the four men on horseback approach from the rear, and now his rosy cheeks lost most of their color as he looked up at Jake Slater, Danny Reeves, Shorty Lockman, and the half-breed, Charlie One-Jump.

"Good afternoon, gentlemen," he replied, retrieving his bowler hat from the wheel of a nearby wagon and placing it gingerly on his head. "G. L. Standish, at your service. Professional photographer, traveler to the far reaches of civilization, and chronicler of the unusual and the bizarre. I've even made an ordinary housewife look good a time or two. How may I tend to your needs, whatever they may be?"

There was a showman's air about G. L. Standish, and with his corpulent frame encased in a vested suit, with a sparkling watchfob dangling across his ample stomach, he looked equally as prepared to sell snake oil as he was to preserve the image of his clients for the pleasure of future generations.

"What the fuck did he say?" Slater asked in a low growl as he glanced across at Reeves.

"He said he'd like to take our picture. Ain't that right, Mr. Standish?"

"I like you, young man," Standish replied, hustling forward to hold his hands up in the form of a square and center them on Reeves's face. "Photogenic is the word used commonly by practitioners of the craft. And that you are. Photogenic. Your face, properly photographed by yours truly, of course, could be embodiment of the frontier spirit."

Obviously irritated by the senseless gibberish of the photographer, Slater nodded toward the wagon before Reeves could offer a response. "What the hell ya got in there?"

"In there, my friend? That is a mobile, yes, I say mobile, darkroom. That fine contrivance was designed and built by none other than the honorable John Mason of Kansas City, and through its portals have passed the likenesses of some of the most beautiful women in the western hemisphere. Not to mention judges, potentates, ambassadors, and other dignitaries too numerous to mention. Won't you be so kind as to look for yourself, sir?" Standish asked, taking a sprightly step toward the curtained opening. "I have no prints in the bath at this present moment, and no harm can be done."

Slater merely grunted in reply, swung down from his saddle, and sauntered to the rear of the wagon to throw the curtain roughly aside. He peered into the gloom for several seconds before turning toward Standish again.

"Can't see a goddamned thing in there. What the hell you use that for?"

"Developing photographs, and as a sleeping accommodation. At high noon on the brightest day of glorious summer, I can ensconce myself within that chamber, and not one iota of light will permeate those solitary quarters."

"Should do the trick, Reeves," Slater said, brushing past the photographer to examine his camera. "This thing work?"

"Work is for the slaves of society, sir," Standish gushed, rushing forward to lay a protective hand on the wooden box suspended upon a tripod. "This marvelous instrument is designed to do away with the work of brush, paint, and pallette, and thereby capture a reasonable likeness in a fraction of the time an old-fashioned portrait artist would require. In thirty minutes you can personally hold the image of your soul in your very own hand."

"Yeah?" Slater said with his brows arched in disbelief. "Show me."

"You ain't got no soul, Jake," Lockman said with a chuckle.

"Shut up, Shorty. Leastwise I'm tall enough to look into the damned thing," Slater replied, lifting the cloth to peer into the open rear end of the camera. "There ain't nothin' on the other side of this but weeds and a burned-out old homesteader's cabin," he said suspiciously.

"Perhaps that's true, but viewed through the artist's eye, this dismal scene is the embodiment of dreams gone awry, the pitiful remains of an empire lost, and the brutality of life in its purist form."

"Pure horseshit, you mean. The goddamned place burned down and the ignorant sonofabitch who built it there got what he deserved. Now, like I said afore, I want to see how this damned thing works. You get down here, Shorty, and learn somethin'," Slater said with a backward glance toward Lockman. "You're gonna need it afore the day is out."

Standish cleared his throat nervously and loosened his collar with the twist of a finger. "Well, sir, perhaps in the enthusiasm of the moment at the sight of my fellow man, I forgot to mention one detail: There is a slight charge for my services."

"Slight charge, your ass! I said I want to see it work and I want to see it work now! We ain't got all day to fuck around here listenin' to your highfalutin' horseshit! Now if you don't understand plain English," Slater snarled, pulling out his Colt .44 and pressing its muzzle against the soft white flesh of Standish's throat, "then maybe you'll understand that this ain't no slingshot, and I've got the patience of a rattlesnake with a man's boot on its tail. Do whatever you do, but I want to see a goddamned picture!"

Standish's eyes bulged, and he swallowed cautiously several times. "Of course, sir. Obviously there has been a slight misunderstanding here. For you there is no charge, no charge at all. Pleasure is the word, my friend—pleasure. It would be my pleasure to present you, free of charge, a photograph taken of yourself and developed by the very hand of G. L. Standish himself."

"Now that's more like it," Slater grunted, holstering his Colt and brushing his mustache back along his cheeks. "With the exception of the occasional whorehouse, J. D. Slater ain't really in the habit of payin' for nothin', if you know what I mean."

"Precisely, Mr. Slater," Standish exclaimed, scurrying to a position about fifteen feet in front of the camera. "I understand precisely. Now if you'll just step over here, sir, I'll position you correctly and then prepare my equipment. With your co-operation, the entire session will take less than five minutes."

Slater moved to the assigned place and watched with a grudging scowl as Standish made several corrections beneath the cloth, adjusted and readjusted the black box, then began pouring silvery powder from a bottle into a steel trough attached to a wooden handle.

Seeing the powder, Slater's scowl turned to a look of defensive concern and he said, "What the hell's that for, mister? You ain't shootin' no damned cannon at me."

Standish laughed a bit nervously, and hastened to reassure the surly Slater. "Of *course* not, sir. This is a flash tray, and I have loaded it with magnesium powder. After I open the camera's shutter, I shall ignite the powder. A brilliant flash will result that will eliminate any shadows."

Slater blinked uncomprehendingly. "Shorty," he called out, "are you watchin' all this?"

"Yessir, boss," Shorty replied, standing on his tiptoes to observe the operation. "But since he don't seem to speak English, I got no idea what he's talkin' about."

"Never fear," Standish offered with a confident smile, replacing the lid on the bottle. "What I have to say is far inferior to what I intend to prove momentarily. Now, if you would be so kind as to stand back, sir," he said, touching Shorty's chest lightly, "and if you, sir, would please remain in that exact position," he continued, nodding toward Slater as he ducked under the cloth, "your image will be immortalized before you can say Jack Robinson."

With that, Standish groped for a rubber bulb dangling from a cord attached to the tripod, held it high above the camera, then froze in position.

"Perfect! Hold that pose, now!"

He squeezed the bulb, and a flat *whump* accompanied the explosion of light atop the flash tray. Slater staggered backward, clawing for his revolver and tripping over his own feet. He went sprawling onto his back.

"Somebody get that sonofabitch!" he yelled.

The other three men merely grinned as Standish emerged from beneath the cloth to study his disoriented subject. There was a look of sweet sorrow on his face as he said, "Now that is too bad. You moved, sir. We'll have to shoot it over again."

"Like hell we will!" Slater snarled, scrambling to his feet, then stooping to retrieve his hat and gun from the dirt. "That's all done and be damned with it! Let's get on with what we came here for!"

"And what would that be, gentlemen?" the photographer asked, turning to look at the two men still mounted.

Reeves crossed his hands over his saddlehorn and looked down at Standish with a pleasant smile. "We came here to offer you a job."

"I see," Standish mused. "And what type of employment would that be? To be frank with you, I'm quite unaccustomed to physical labor."

"That's not what I'm talking about," Reeves countered. "We just want you to take some pictures for us, that's all."

"Precisely my line of work. You do intend to pay for my services?"

"Of course, and we'll be generous, to boot."

"How generous?"

"Fifty dollars, cash money, for three hours' work, but that includes you, your camera, and your wagon over there."

Standish smiled slyly and nodded while pressing his fingertips together before his chest. "I see. A considerable sum for the hours required." He turned his saintly gaze on Reeves and added, "So considerable that I detect something slightly illegal underfoot."

"Naw, nothin' like that. But it does have to be done slick-like and kept a secret, just amongst the five of us."

"Very well," Standish said. "Please explain."

"It's like this," Slater replied. "My intended bride is bein' held against her will at an army post hereabouts. Her ma and pa had the army kidnap her away from me—they're real rich folks and can do stuff like that. She went a little crazy when they took her away from me, so she might get a little wild and

127

unreasonable when she sees us, but don't pay that no mind. Anyways, we come up with a way to get her out of there, and that's where you come in..."

Lieutenant Morris rode between Matt Kincaid and Windy Mandalian at the head of the twin columns as they worked their way toward the Sioux reservation. The sun had now climbed well above the horizon, and the chill of dawn had been replaced by the first intimations of another sultry day on the High Plains.

Kincaid looked across at Morris and said, "How's the arm?"

Morris looked down at the arm in its sling, resting across his chest, and shook his head. "Useless, sir, even though you and Windy did a fine job of setting it. I certainly can't perform an operation with it."

"I won't ask you to," Kincaid replied, "but the operation has to be done. A good many lives are at stake besides that Indian boy's."

"But who's going to do it?" Morris asked, dumbfounded.

"I am," Kincaid said softly, staring between his horse's ears at the low range of prairie swells in the distance that sheltered the Sioux encampment.

"You, sir?" Morris asked in surprise. "I mean no disrespect, Lieutenant, but an appendectomy is no simple matter."

"How many have *you* done?"

"Well... none. But I've been trained in the procedure. That makes quite a difference, and I have removed the appendixes on numerous cadavers."

"The liklihood of another cadaver, with or without appendix, is what we are coming here to prevent, Lieutenant," Kincaid said firmly. "I held the book for you last time, you hold it for me this time. You tell me what to do and I'll do it. Just because your arm is broken, that doesn't mean you can't speak. We have to do the best we can with what we have, and at this moment that arrangement seems to be the best we can come up with."

"Don't think so, Matt," Windy said, reining his horse around a gully and then swinging in beside Morris once more. "Least not in the order you just said."

"What do you mean by that, Windy?"

The scout chewed his lump of cut-plug in thought before replying. "I've been around a skinnin' knife a lot more'n you have, and I'd venture to say I've cut holes in people a few more times, as well. Not that they were likin' it, you understand. Anyway, I'm pretty steady when it comes to holdin' a knife, even a tiny little one like the doc here uses. Seems we've got a lot ridin' on this, and it all comes down to the best man with a knife in a bad situation."

"This is beyond belief!" Morris protested. "We're not talking about skinning a damned buffalo! We're talking about delicate surgery, for God's sake!"

Windy squinted as he took in the lieutenant's exasperated look. "Son, I can take this old bowie here and skin a buff's eye without drawin' blood. Ain't no surgery can get more delicate than that."

"Do you realize what you're doing, Windy?" Kincaid asked, dismissing Morris entirely. "If the boy dies, you're in this as deeply as I am."

"I know that, Matt," the scout replied, nodding toward the warriors riding out to intercept them. "You always did need somebody to cover your backside anyway. "Here comes the greetin' party. Let's act like we know what we're doin', even if we don't. 'Bout this business—I saw an old Canuck doctor take one out of a breed Frenchman one time up in Canada a few years back. Simple as shootin' the balls off a squirel, seemed to me like."

Morris could do nothing more than shake his head in disbelief, then watch apprehensively as they were surrounded by fierce-looking Sioux warriors.

Seated as he had been during the night, Kills Many Bear watched them approach. Were it not for the transition from dark to light and a dying fire before him, it would have seemed that nothing had changed. His back remained turned to the tipi opening just behind him, Beaver Claw stood off to one side; the village had a distinct aura of mourning about it. Kincaid, Mandalian, and Morris dismounted and approached the chief, who slowly rose from his blankets.

"I have broken my promise to you," Kincaid said evenly. "I said we would return by the rising of the sun, and now it is well into the heavens."

Kills Many Bear allowed no change of expression. "You have returned. That was your promise."

"Thank you, Chief. I have also brought the doctor, as promised. How is your son?"

"He is alive, but his spirit will soon go."

"Maybe not," Kincaid replied, controlling a sigh of relief. "This is Lieutenant Morris. He is an army doctor, trained in such matters like the young Sioux are trained in the manhood ritual. He will do all that can be done for your son."

Kills Many Bear's eyes shifted slowly to Morris's face, and he seemed not to notice the arm dangling in its sling. "You bring medicine?"

"Well . . . ah . . . yes. Yes, Chief, I did," Morris stammered, raising his black bag for the Indian to see. "The medicine is in here."

"That is good. Go to my son. If he dies, so will the lieutenant. That was our agreement."

Morris whirled in astonishment. "What? What the hell's he mean by that?"

"Nothing," Kincaid muttered through gritted teeth. "It's just a promise I made in a moment of weakness. Tell the chief that you must be left alone with only the two of us to help you."

"This is craz—"

"Do it!"

"I . . . I will go to your son now," Morris said weakly, even though his knuckles were white on the bag handle. "I must be left completely alone, with the exception of Mr. Mandalian and Lieutenant Kincaid. And I will need boiling water."

Kills Many Bear watched them in silence before nodding. "You will have water. Go now."

The three white men filed past the chief. Stooping, they entered the tipi to see Striking Hawk lying there, his chest barely rising with each shallow breath. Instantly, total composure swept over Morris at the sight of the dying man and he knelt quickly to feel for a pulse. Satisfied, he turned and looked up at the men standing over him.

"His pulse rate is slow but strong, which is good, if we do have to operate. It will minimize the flow of blood."

Then he turned back and lifted the pelt from Striking Hawk's stomach, laid it across the Indian's thighs, and then began a gentle probing of the lower abdomen. Nearly two minutes had passed before he glanced up again.

"Whoever diagnosed this for you was correct; the appendix will have to come out. Open my bag there and get the carbolic acid, a bottle of ether, and the small packet containing my surgical equipment. When the water comes, mix—"

"I know," Kincaid said with a grin, "one part carbolic acid to three parts of water in one container and three parts to thirty in the other. I went through the first one with you, remember?"

"Yes, I guess you did, sir. Then you'll know how to administer the ether too?"

"Yes. I might need a little help remembering when to apply it, but you'll take care of that, I'm sure. Did you bring your medical book?" Kincaid asked as a squaw entered carrying two containers of water, which she set down near the fire.

"Yes, it's in my saddlebag, sir. Please—"

"Forget the 'sir' for now. We're partners in this together."

Morris's tone instantly became professional. "Get the book from my saddlebags and turn it to the section on abdominal diseases and injuries. While you're doing that, Windy and I can sterilize our hands, then he can sterilize the instruments while I cleanse the incision area."

"Right," Kincaid replied, moving toward the entranceway.

"Windy? When we wash, be sure and clean real well under your fingernails. That's very important. Then, when your hands are throughly sterilized, don't touch anything except the instruments and body parts. I'll do the same with my left hand, just in case you need some assistance."

"You're the doctor," Windy replied simply. "Ain't never had to do this for a buff, but then, none of them buff ever walked again, either."

Morris looked at Windy closely and began to recount surgical procedure for an appendectomy, with an occasional glance at the medical book. "First we'll have to make an incision about three inches long at an oblique angle, so we split the peritoneum rather than sever it. I'll show you where to cut so we don't make any mistakes. The appendix is a small, pencil-like structure connected with the cecum, the first part of the large intestine. You'll see that as we go in, and—"

"Yeah. I'm sure I will."

"Don't worry about it. I know what they look like. The important thing is to cauterize each blood vessel attached to the appendix immediately after we sever it! The cauterizing instrument will be kept hot in the coals at all times, and I can hand it to you when needed. After we've severed all the blood vessels, we detach the appendix from the cecum and lift it free. I'm certain we're dealing with acute appendicitis here, but I don't think, judging from the appearance of things, that we have peritonitis, which is a rupture of the appendix due to excessive swelling. We'll see when we get in there. The appendix is normally pearly white in color, but it will tend to discolor as the disease progresses. There is usually a dark spot in the fatty tissue where the pressure is greatest, and if that has burst, then we're in over our heads."

Mandalian glanced at Kincaid with a wry smile. "But not until then." Then he looked at Morris again. "Hell, Doc, forget the schoolhouse lessons. I can't understand a damned thing you've said so far, anyway. Show me where to cut, what to do, and let's get on with it."

"Just like shooting the balls off a squirrel, huh, Windy?" Kincaid asked with a grin.

"Yup. But this is a damned small squirrel."

"All right, but once we start, there's no turning back. Lieutenant? Pour some ether on that cloth—several drops should do it—then press it lightly over the patient's nose. By the time it takes effect, I will have shown Windy where to cut," Morris said, taking up the scapel and handing it to the scout, who looked down at the tiny cutting instrument dwarfed by his big hands, and gripped it uncomfortably as he would have a big knife.

"No, Windy. Hold it like you would a pencil, and use the flat of your palm with your little finger spread out like this"— he demonstrated with his left hand—"and that finger will serve as a guide along the abdomen so the scalpel doesn't slip."

"Think maybe we should've used the bowie," Windy replied, testing the technique awkwardly.

"Or maybe an ax," Morris rejoined with a slight smile. Then he leaned forward and traced a line across Striking Hawk's abdomen. "We'll make the incision here, Windy. Use a light touch, because we'll want to layer our way into and through the peritoneum. I'll help dab the blood away as we go." He looked up at Kincaid. "Is he out?"

"Beats hell out of me. How do I tell?"

"Lift the eyelids. If there is no reflex blink, and the eyes don't waver in any direction, he's out."

Kincaid did this and said, "I'd say he's out."

"Good. Watch for those signs throughout the surgery. If they occur we'll know we're not using enough ether and have to administer more. Too much can be worse than too little, though, unfortunately. Are you ready, Windy?"

"Yup."

"Then start the incision."

The tiny surgical blade lowered to soft, bronzed skin, hesitated once, then touched flesh to be drawn deftly along the line indicated by Morris. Windy's hand was steady, and when

132

he lifted the blade away, a gash a quarter-inch deep and three inches long had been made and blood rose to the surface, which Morris dabbed away. Even though the Indian was lean, there was a layer of fat beneath the skin that showed alternately white and red as the doctor continued to sponge up blood and examine the incision.

"Perfect, Windy. You're just above the peritoneum now. Cut through the muscle carefully, and then we'll spread it apart with clamps. After that, we should be into the area of the stomach cavity and be able to see the cecum."

Windy nodded and again the scalpel went down, dipping into the incision.

After the third repetition, Morris said, "Hold it, Windy, I think we're through. Yes, I know we are. I think I can handle the clamps with my left hand," he continued, working as he talked. "You keep dabbing that blood away. That's good. Real good. There, we've got them in place. That large, round, fatty-looking object is the cecum. And there, at the very end of it, is the appendix. See it?"

"Yeah, Doc, I see it. Is that dinky little son of a bitch causin' all this trouble?"

"A very painful thing, appendicitis," Morris murmured, studying the appendix. "It's quite badly discolored, but it hasn't burst, so at least we're not looking at peritonitis. Let's get it out. How's that ether doing, Lieutenant?"

"Seems to be about right, Doc."

"Good. This whole procedure will take roughly an hour, so keep a close watch on him. We've been at it a good fifteen minutes already. Windy, you're on your own from here on, so to speak. There's not enough room for my hand and yours as well. Feel along the appendix with your index finger, and you should be able to locate the blood vessels. After you've cut one, nod and I'll cauterize."

Working slowly, deftly, Mandalian found and severed each of the blood vessels, then nodded and spread his fingers apart for the red-hot tip of the instrument to pass between them. Another twenty minutes passed in total silence until Windy made one last searching probe.

"Feels like we got 'em all, Doc."

"Good Now disconnect the appendix from the cecum and when you have, lift it out quickly, because I'll have to cauterize the point of separation."

With studied concentration, Windy found the point of connection, took a half breath, then severed the appendix from the cecum and lifted out a small, twisted object that resembled a section of white rope with two bends in it. Quickly, Morris pressed the cauterizing instrument into the opening and there was a faint odor of burned flesh momentarily before he stepped back.

"Nice work, Windy. We'll leave the cavity open for a few minutes to make sure there is no internal bleeding, and then we'll close. To do that, we'll use this hooked needle and catgut thread. The peritoneum will heal itself, and we'll only stitch the surface skin."

"Sounds good to me. What the hell do I do with this?" Mandalian asked, offering the appendix held between two bloody fingers.

"Just lay it aside for now. I've got a jar of formaldehyde in my bag. I'll take it with me to examine later."

When Morris was absolutely certain that the cauterization had been successful, he removed the clamps and washed the incision throughly with carbolic acid solution before saying to Kincaid, "No more ether, Lieutenant. By the time he comes out of it, we'll be through here."

Taking up the threaded needle, the doctor held it up for Windy to see. "Have you ever done any stitching, Windy?"

"Yup. Made a lot of moccasins in my day."

"Fine. Use the same technique. Insert the needle on one side of the incision, press it through to the other side, then pull the catgut all the way through, leaving about two inches to spare. We'll tie that end off and proceed along, looping over just like you were following the curvature of the needle. Should take about twenty stitches, then we'll tie the far end off." Morris paused to look at the comatose Sioux. "If he lives, I'll come back in a few days and take the stitches out."

"Whaddaya mean, if he lives?" Windy asked hotly. "Hell, boy, ain't no patient of mine gonna die on me. I'm gonna have him sewed up like a goose ready for roastin'. Give me that there needle, son, and stand back."

In response to the doctor's questioning glance, Kincaid merely shrugged his shoulders and grinned as Mandalian bent to his work. When the last bit of catgut had been expertly tied off with a fishing knot, he stood back to examine his work.

"She may not be purty," he said pridefully, "but I'll damned sure betcha she ain't gonna leak."

Kincaid chuckled and Morris allowed a tentative smile, then bent forward to bathe the stitches and incision with carbolic again, while Matt and Windy cleansed the surgical instruments. After the blood had been washed away and the equipment packed in the bag once more, the three men looked down intently at the young Indian's face.

"Come on, son, blink them eyes," Mandalian said softly. "You can't let me down. Just think of all them purty little squaws you've got yet to fuck. After you show 'em our scar, of course."

"He should be coming out of it any time now, Windy," Morris responded professionally, leaning down to lift an eyelid, which twitched under his thumb. Several minutes later, both eyelids fluttered, then opened, and Striking Hawk looked up at the strange white doctor bending over him.

"You're going to be all right, son. You were a mighty sick young man, but you're going to be just fine now. We just removed your appendix, which was causing the pain, and to do that we used a form of anesthesia called ether. It'll make you feel nauseated for a while, but that'll go away quickly."

Striking Hawk stared blankly at Morris, then rolled his head toward Kincaid and Windy.

"Howdy, Striking Hawk," Windy said with a broad smile. "What the doctor there is trying to say is, give it a day or two and you'll be kickin' the shit out of the Crow again."

Even though confused, the young Indian blinked his eyes several times and lifted his head testingly to look down at where the pain had been, which had now been replaced by a dull ache.

"That's where your appendix was," Morris said, taking up the vial of formaldehyde and showing it to Striking Hawk. "And this is where it is now. This is what was making you sick. I want you to lie still for a day or two. Sure, you can move your arms and your head, but don't lift your legs or try to sit up."

"Can I bring the chief in now, Doctor?" Kincaid asked. "Is the boy well enough?"

"Sure. Bring him in for a few minutes, then we'd better go outside if we want to talk."

Kincaid moved through the opening and returned with Kills Many Bear, who stepped inside and looked toward his son. Striking Hawk raised his head again and nodded toward the stitches. They exchanged words in Sioux, the young man laid his head down again, and Kills Many Bear nodded his satisfaction as he turned and left the tipi.

Kincaid and Mandalian followed him outside, while Morris scooped up his medical bag. As they stepped into the sunlight, Beaver Claw faced them with a glower, and numerous braves stood behind him.

"My son will not die," Kills Many Bear said with no indication of emotion. "He has told me this with his own tongue."

"Your son had no white man's curse, Kills Many Bear," Kincaid said, taking the vial from Morris's hand with a glance at Beaver Claw. "This is what made Striking Hawk ill, not a white man's curse. It is called an appendix, and it would have killed Striking Hawk if the white doctor had not taken it out."

A murmur swept through the braves standing behind Beaver Claw, and the medicine chief stepped forward angrily. "It is a lie! The white doctor brought this . . . thing with him. They have tricked the Sioux before, and they will trick us again with lies like this. Do not let your eyes be blinded by these lies."

The medicine chief's face was livid with rage, and he turned on Kills Many Bear. "The white men have taken everything from us—our land, our freedom, our weapons, our buffalo and elk. Now they want to steal our medicine too! You are a fool, Kills Many Bear! An old fool! They cannot steal our medicine from us with tricks like this! Our medicine is a sacred thing, and we will fight to keep it even if we cannot win!"

With those words, Beaver Claw spun on his heel and stalked away with several of his followers hesitating at first, then following close behind. Kills Many Bear watched the medicine chief go before turning to Kincaid.

"We made an agreement. You are free to go."

"Thank you for your trust in me, chief. The reason we were late getting here this morning is that we were attacked by Sioux. Some of my men were wounded, including the doctor here. The other men have been taken to the agency. Three warriors were killed. Our agreement also included keeping your people on the reservation until I can find the men who are causing this trouble between our people. Can you keep that agreement?"

The old chief nodded. "I can keep the agreement for those who follow me."

"And those who don't?"

"That the gods must decide. To save my son, I have done

a bad thing for my people. I have brought shame on our medicine chiefs and they are angry. The gods will guide me, or punish me. They will make the decision."

"I see. If there must be war between yourself and Beaver Claw, so be it. Do not let innocent Sioux be killed by taking your fight away from the reservation. I will catch the guilty ones who killed your two warriors, and they will be punished in the white man's way. Do not let war happen between us because of them, my friend."

Kills Many Bear stared stoically into the distance for nearly a full minute before offering a reply. "You came here in peace and you leave here in peace. I will do what the gods decide. My heart goes with you for what you have done for my son."

There was nothing more to be said, and the three white men returned to their mounts.

"I hope the gods decide in our favor, Matt," Windy said with a grunt as he swung onto his saddle. Kincaid was already mounted, and he turned his horse away. "Me too, but I've got a hunch Beaver Claw is going to hear a little different message than our friend over there, Windy. Corporal Miller?"

"Yes, sir?"

"We'll be going back to the agency to pick up those wounded men Corporal Wojensky took there this morning. A couple of them were shot up pretty bad, and I want the doctor to check them over before we start back to the post."

"Yes, sir. *Squaaaad! Fall into ranks!*"

Lieutenant Morris had finally managed to mount his horse, and he urged the animal up beside Kincaid's. "I'd like to congratulate both of you on a fine job back there," he said. "It may not have been first-rate surgery, but it was the best that could be done under the circumstances."

"The boy's alive. That's all that matters."

"Actually," Morris continued, "I was rather pleased with our accomplishment, but that Beaver Claw fellow didn't quite seem to see it that way."

"No, he didn't. He had the look of war in his eyes," Kincaid replied.

"Wasn't that the idea behind saving the boy's life in the first place? To prevent war?"

"It was, and it still is. Kills Many Bear has a tough hand to draw to, but he'll do the best he can to honor our agreement."

"And if he doesn't?"

Kincaid smiled bitterly. "Then you'll have to learn to operate with one hand damned quick. You'll have plenty of work to do."

Windy sliced off a chunk of cut-plug and nestled it in his cheek. "And you'll have to learn to do your own cuttin' work by yourself, too, Doc. I can't handle 'er. Gotta be too damned clean, and there ain't no place to spit."

ten

It was about three o'clock in the afternoon when Captain Conway stepped away from the telegraph shack and began moving across the parade with a lengthy telegram in his hand, which he scanned as he walked. There was a look of satisfaction on his face, as though he had found the missing pieces to an intricate jigsaw puzzle, and he began to scrutinize the yellow sheet of paper more closely, glancing up occasionally to return a salute, then looking down at the telegram once again. He was thoroughly engrossed in the document, and when he heard his name called, his head jerked up abruptly like that of a man jolted from a deep sleep.

"Captain Conway?"

Conway glanced in the direction of the main gate, where the call had come from. "Yes, Corporal? What is it?"

"There's a couple of men out here requesting permission to enter the post, sir!"

Conway took several steps to the right to gain a clearer view, and he saw a strangely designed wagon. Two men watched him from the driver's seat, and he could see that one was a large, fat man while the other was short of stature and slimly built.

"Did they state the nature of their business, Corporal?"

"Yes, sir. They said they wanted to, uh, take some pictures," the sentry replied.

"Allow them entry, Corporal. I'll talk with them here." Conway's eyes went back to the telegram once more, while the wagon creaked forward, and he didn't glance up again until the conveyance had stopped beside him.

"Can I help you gentlemen with something?"

"Indeed you can, sir," the big man said, beaming down from above while he swept the bowler hat from his head. "Allow me to introduce myself. I am G. L. Standish and this is my trusted companion, Shorty Lockman."

"Pleased to meet you gentlemen, I'm sure," Conway replied with a smile, secretly amused at the oddity of the pair. "I'm Captain Conway. What can I do for you?"

"Ah! 'Tis not what you can do for us, sir, but rather what we can do for you."

"And what would that be?"

"We have arrived to immortalize you and the men of your command forever. I, sir, have been commissioned by the federal government to travel at length throughout this far-flung nation of ours to photograph installations such as this one for documentation purposes. As I'm sure you are well aware, there are some, shall we say, doubting-Thomases back East who question the expense of maintaining these military outposts, and it is the intention of the War Department to show up those doubts for the falsehoods they truly are."

Conway watched Standish quizzically. "Let me get this straight. You were sent here to take pictures of this outpost by the War Department?"

"Precisely!" Standish boomed enthusiastically.

"And you have orders to that effect, I presume?"

"Not exactly, sir," Standish replied, throwing his hands up in mock dispair. "You, perhaps more than anyone else, should know how difficult such an acquisition can be. I am merely a poor merchant dealing in the art of photography who has taken this monumental but patriotic task upon himself on a consignment basis. At great personal expense, I might add."

"I see," Conway replied absently, anxious to excuse himself from this ridiculous conversation and get back to the telegram and its meaning in the solitude of his office. "That sounds harmless enough. What do you want from me?"

"You are most kind, sir. I ask merely to be allowed to set up my photographic equipment and capture this moment in history," Standish said with an evaluating glance at the lowering sun, "before we lose the proper light. I have far to travel this night, and I must leave once my task is completed. When the sun has sunk to its well earned rest, G. L. Standish shall be gone. There are others who require my services and deserve them equally as much as yourself."

Conway couldn't resist a chuckle at the man's bombastic language. "Help yourselves. If there's anything you need, just let someone know," he said, starting to move away. "I have work to do, but I'm certain that one of my junior officers would be more than glad to help."

"Far be it from me to disturb a man on a mission of such importance as yours, sir. You have been most generous. If you would be so kind as to allow me to rest my weary horses in that shade over there," Standish continued, pointing toward the shaded area in front of the bachelor officer's quarters, "I would be forever in your debt. That will avail me of the proper light from behind and simplify my task greatly."

"Be my guest," Conway said with a shrug, as his eyes went again to the telegram.

"Thank you, sir," Standish called after the receding captain.

Conway merely shook his head once more and continued to walk toward his office. He didn't see the sly look of cunning victory on Standish's face, nor did he notice the triumphant jab of Standish's elbow into the ribs of the little man beside him. Taking the reins once again, Standish positioned the wagon exactly as Reeves had instructed him to do, then climbed down from the seat with studied effort.

"Now, my friend," Standish said to Shorty, who had jumped down and rounded the end of the wagon, "while I get my equipment in position, you circle within the walls and let the good people know we're here."

With a satisfied smile, Standish began preparing for a photographic session while Shorty passed among the off-duty soldiers lounging about in the shade.

"Get your picture taken by the great, the one and only G. L. Standish! Send them to your wife, send them to your children, send them to your loved ones! Get your picture taken now! A once-in-a-lifetime opportunity! G. L. Standish himself will take your photograph!"

By the time he had reached the sutler's store, a crowd had already begun to form, and once the ladies shopping within heard Shorty's cry, they hustled toward their quarters to deposit packages and primp for an unusual event on the frontier. And when he finally completed his rounds, the flash tray had already sent up its first puff of smoke, with Standish constantly repeating in a gleeful tone:

"Just drop your dollar in the hat, please. Form an orderly line now, ladies and gentlemen, and drop your dollar in the hat when it's your turn. Smile now! That's good! Thank you! Next, please!"

Flora Conway passed along beneath the awning, and paused to watch the show while smiling in disbelief at the enthusiasm displayed by soldiers and their ladies alike over the opportunity to have their pictures taken. Then she opened the dispensary door and stepped inside.

"Hello, Lee Ellen," she offered pleasantly, placing the bundle of cloth she held in her arms upon a nearby table. "How are you feeling this afternoon?"

"Fine, Flora, thank you. Have you heard anything about Frederick?"

"No, I haven't, dear. But he'll be just fine, I'm sure of that. He's with Windy and Lieutenant Kincaid, and they'll make sure he gets back to you. I don't blame you for your concern though; I felt the same way when Warner went away on patrol for the first time," Flora said, gazing at the wall with a wistful look in her eyes. "But he came back, as he always has. A little worse for wear, maybe, but he's always come back."

"I suppose it is foolish of me to worry," Lee Ellen said with lowered eyelids, "but he is the kindest, most gentle man I have ever known. He hasn't told me he cares for me yet, but I think he does."

"Of course he does. How could he resist? Just give him time to find his tongue, that's all. Men are strange that way, but they come around eventually. And after he sees you in this," Flora said brightly, turning to hold a length of patterned fabric across her narrow waist, "he'll be like an infant child in your hands."

Lee Ellen stared at the material in disbelief. "What do you mean, after he sees me in this? I don't understand."

"This is the material I'm going to use to make a new dress for you, silly," Flora replied, laying the cloth across Lee Ellen's shoulder to see how it would look on her. "It will be absolutely gorgeous with your dark hair."

"For me? This is for me? You're going to make a dress for me?"

"Of course I am, and Maggie's going to help. We want to do it for you, Lee Ellen," Flora said softly. "You didn't have much when you arrived here."

"Oh, it's beautiful. Absolutely beautiful!" Lee Ellen exclaimed, touching the material to her cheek before reaching out with her right hand to hug Flora the best she could. "I just can't wait to see it!"

"Neither can I, but we'll just have to wait. Anticipation is the best part of a gift, I suppose. I wish we had it done, though, and you were well enough to walk. There's a photographer taking pictures outside right now, and I'd love to have a picture of you wearing a dress made of this material."

Lee Ellen glanced toward the shuttered window. "Is that what all the commotion is about out there?"

"Yes. It seems everybody on the post is lined up to have his picture taken except you and me."

"No, I'd rather wait," Lee Ellen said firmly, gazing at the wall with a determined stare. "I'll wait until Frederick and I can have our picture taken together. With me in this dress and him in his uniform. He is handsome, don't you think?" she asked, turning again to look at Flora.

"Very much so. Now, I've got to go and prepare Warner's supper. I'll look in on you again just before dark. All right?"

"Yes, and thank you so much for the beautiful thought," Lee Ellen said, hugging the material one last time before Flora gently took it away. "I'll do something nice for you someday, you just wait and see."

"You already have, Lee Ellen. You've allowed me to be your friend and have accepted my friendship in return. That's the nicest thing you could have done for me. Get some rest now, and I'll be back before dark to light a lamp for you."

"Thanks, Flora. You're very kind," Lee Ellen said, resting her head again on the pillow to lose herself in thoughts about the new dress and how special she would look for the young lieutenant the first time he saw her wearing it.

With the camera focused on a stool situated some fifteen feet from the lens, it was a simple process to tilt the box at whatever angle the person's height required, then squeeze the bulb, a job that Standish relegated to Shorty while he developed the prints in his mobile darkroom. Each time Standish came out of the wagon with a developed picture, Shorty had another plate ready for processing, and as the afternoon wore on they managed to take photographs of nearly everyone who desired them. But with the sun sinking lower, Standish came out with his final print, and despite groans of disappointment, he dismissed the few unlucky patrons remaining. Pausing to retrieve his hat with possibly thirty dollars collected, Standish instructed Shorty in the proper procedure for dismantling the camera, and by the time twilight settled over the post, the equipment was again loaded into the wagon.

"It will be totally dark in about fifteen minutes," Standish said to the two men huddled inside the cramped wagon as he washed his last plate. "When I'm through here, I'll go outside, and when the time is right, I'll tap three times on the side of the wagon and the two of you can execute your humanitarian deed."

"'Bout goddamned time," Slater growled as he tried to stretch his legs. "Seems like I've been cooped up in this crowded son of a bitch since Hector was a pup."

"Shhhh. Keep your voice down," Standish admonished him. "Patience is a virtue, and all things come in good time. We've had a thriving business here today. This is a source of revenue that I seem to have completely overlooked, and I thank you gentlemen for having corrected that oversight."

"Shut up. Get outside and see what the hell's goin' on."

Standish heaved his considerable bulk through the rear door of the wagon and let the curtain drop just as Conway stepped from his office.

"Good evening to you, sir," the photographer said innocently, while frantically tugging the curtain down behind him. "May I offer my most sincere gratitude for the fine thing you've done here today. Not only have you made numerous people happy, you have also served your government well."

Conway yawned and rubbed the back of his neck to ease

the muscles, while surveying the sky. "You're welcome Mr. Standish. I'm happy to serve in any way I can," he added with a wry smile. "Did you get everything you had hoped to get?"

"Not quite yet, Captain," Standish replied with a disarming smile. "But I am certain I shall leave totally satisfied." Then, catching himself, he added, "By that I mean I had hoped to have the pleasure of photographing you, sir. Perhaps another time."

"Yes, perhaps another time. Right now I'm ready for some dinner and a cigar. It's been a long day."

"Then, please, sir, don't let me detain you. I shall be leaving within the half hour and my gratitude shall forever keep me in your debt."

"Forget it. Good night and have a safe journey," Conway said, moving away in the manner of a man who had just been freed from a bog.

"And a pleasant good night to you, sir."

When darkness had completely settled in, Standish looked in both directions, then gently tapped his code on the side of the wagon. He heard the scraping of boots from within, then looked over his shoulder one more time and saw a woman walking toward him beneath the awning.

"Not yet!" Standish said sharply, and the movement behind him stopped while the photographer quickly doffed his hat and passed it across his waist in a sweeping bow.

"Good evening, ma'am. A pleasant one for you, I hope."

Flora hesitated before the door of Morris's quarters and looked at Standish quizzically for a moment. "Were you talking to me?"

"I most certainly was, my dear. I wished you—"

"No, I mean before that. You said 'not yet,' or words to that effect."

"Oh, that," Standish replied, thinking rapidly. "Yes, of course. I was speaking to my assistant. He was about to drive off before I had our equipment properly secured. Isn't it a shame what absolutely abominable help a person has to put up with these days?"

"I wouldn't know. I've never had to put up with any. Good night to you, sir."

"And good evening to you, ma'am."

After one last queer look at the photographer, Flora stepped inside, and when the door closed, Standish leaned heavily against the wagon while fanning his face rapidly with his hat. Then he scurried to the front of the wagon and knelt down on the far side, as if inspecting a wheel hub. Moments later he saw Flora emerge from the room, close the door behind her, and return to her quarters. He noticed that a lamp had been lit in the room, then tapped on the side of the wagon three times.

In seconds, Slater and Reeves jumped from the wagon and moved quickly into the shadow of the awning. When Reeves came to the door of Lee Ellen's room, he placed a hand on the latch and sprang inside with the quickness of a cat. He crossed the room in three strides, and before he startled Lee Ellen could utter a scream for help, his hand closed over her mouth in a viselike grip.

"Don't say a word, honey," he soothed as Slater moved up beside him. "We'll be going for a little ride now, and your friends won't even know you've left. Come on, Jake. Tie a gag around her mouth quick!"

With the gag in place, they carried Lee Ellen to the door and peered outside before sprinting across the opening and loading Lee Ellen into the back of the wagon. Reeves emerged seconds later to dash into the room once more with an old blanket, which he arranged beneath the bedcovers to make it appear as though Lee Ellen were sleeping. Then he closed the door and leaped into the back of the wagon.

Standish and Shorty were waiting on the front seat, and at the sound of a solid thump against the front wall, the photographer clucked his horses into motion with a simultaneous slap of the reins, and the animals plodded slowly forward. When they reached the far wall, the gates opened before them and the wagon rattled onto the prairie and was soon lost in the darkness.

It was shortly after dawn when the combined squads, with Kincaid, Mandalian, and Morris in the lead, finally passed through the gates of Outpost Number Nine. The weariness of the entire unit was evident in the way their mounts walked— heads drooping, their normally spirited gait reduced to a stumbling shuffle.

Captain Conway was there to greet them as they filed onto the parade, and he laid a hand on the sweat-encrusted withers of Kincaid's horse.

"Welcome home, Matt. Looks like you've had a rough patrol. How many wounded?"

"Four, sir, including Lieutenant Morris here," Kincaid replied with a nod toward the doctor. "I'll give you a full report later, but we were jumped by a Sioux war party. We killed three of them, we saved Striking Hawk's life, and it looks like the Sioux are in for an all-out medicine war, which I think might spill off the reservation."

"Sounds grim, but that's enough for now. We'll talk further when you've had some rest. You and Windy have been in the saddle for quite a while now."

Kincaid offered a weak grin. "Roughly forty-eight hours, sir. And I'm going to forget about the fifteen-minute nap the old bastard had at the agency."

. "Fifteen minutes, hell! If it was more'n five, I'll shine your goddamned boots for a month," Windy said.

"Glad to see everything is normal," Conway observed with a chuckle, while he glanced at Morris. "How are you doing, Doctor? From the look of your arm, I'd say you got a taste of what life's like with a mounted infantry unit a little earlier than either of us had expected."

"It'll heal, sir. If it doesn't, I've got two excellent interns who can look after me," Morris replied, inclining the sling toward Kincaid and Windy.

Slightly confused by the matching grins on the faces of the three, Conway said, "Must be an inside joke. I'm sure I'll hear about it later. Since we're short of room, we'll have the wounded taken to their quarters and treat them there. If you wouldn't mind, Matt, I'd like to see you and Windy in my office for a few minutes before you turn in."

"Of course, sir," Kincaid said, and turned to his corporal. "Corporal Miller? Have the able-bodied help the wounded into the barracks, make sure their mounts are tended to, and then dismiss them."

"Yes, sir."

While the orders were being relayed, Morris looked intently at Kincaid and asked, "May I have permission to go now? I . . . I'd like to look in on my other patient."

"Certainly, Lieutenant. There's nothing more you can do for our military wounded now, so consider yourself dismissed, do what you have to do, and get some rest."

"Thank you, sir," Morris said, dismounting and walking wearily across the parade.

Kincaid and Windy stepped down as well, and after handing the reins of their horses to a waiting private, they followed

Captain Conway toward his office.

"You know, Captain," Kincaid said, "I think the doctor's interest in his patient goes a bit beyond professional concern."

"I suspect you're right," Conway agreed. "There's a slight odor of romance in the air."

They stepped through the orderly room and into Conway's office. Conway turned up the wick on his lamp and gestured to the two empty chairs across from his desk. "Sit down, you two," he said. "How about a bit of brandy? I think you've earned it."

The two men accepted the offer gratefully and sat down, sighing. The captain poured two glasses and handed them across the desk. The men took the drinks and sipped them while Conway spoke.

"Before we get into your report," he said, "I've got some news that might be of interest to you. I've been snooping around a little since you two have been gone, and this telegram here is the most recent development. The last time we talked, Windy mentioned a robbery from which the money was never recovered. The information was difficult to track down, but I was able to find out that the two robbers—who were, in fact, our friends Dugan and Slater—were sent to Leavenworth. I sent a wire to the warden there, and this telegram was his response.

"Now I won't bother wasting your time with a complete reading because I know both of you are damned near out on your feet, but the thing I wanted to tell you is this: They robbed the Bank of Newcastle, a town about a day and a half's ride from here, and close to the Black Hills. Fifty thousand dollars had been secretly deposited there for later shipment to the mines and the only way it could have been known that the money was there was for someone on the inside to have been in on the robbery. That's not so unusual, I suppose, but a bank officer quit abruptly, three days after the robbery. He vanished and they finally gave up looking for him, but he was a principal suspect in this particular case. He had been shot in another robbery, and the bullet took off the lower half of his right ear. He was bitter toward the bank after that, and the reason he became a suspect was his past anger and his sudden departure without any prior notice."

Conway hesitated, looked up from the telegram, and interlaced his fingers, with his elbows propped on the desk. "That man's name was Weston Doberly. Now it's not uncommon for a criminal to want to use a part of his original name when he takes an alias, and if a person had no reason to associate one with another, Weston Doberly would be just another name. But it's just a bit too close to another name that figures in all this business."

The look on Matt Kincaid's face was not one of total shock, but he did show some surprise. "What was the name of that bank that was robbed, sir?"

Conway searched the telegram once more. "It was in a town called Newcastle. Have you got something, Matt?"

"Yes, I believe I have. None of the pieces fit into place until now. While Windy was checking for brand alterations, I went to Dobler's place as you told me to do. He was gone, and I went into his office. The safe was open, so I glanced through his ledger and I was thoroughly surprised at how neat and tidy the columns of figures were. I thought at the time it was unusual for a common rancher to be so precise and fastidious. At the bottom of each column were the initials 'W. D.'"

"That'd fit in with his banking background, Matt," Windy offered.

"Yes, it would, Windy," Kincaid said excitedly. "But there's more. The reason the vault door hadn't closed was that the string from a bank money bag was lying unnoticed outside the safe. I picked the bag up and tried to read the lettering on it. Some of it was too faded to be legible, but from what you've just told us, I think what it might have said was 'Bank of Newcastle.'"

"Don't forget them holes dug all over the northeast corner of his property, and that old Reb you talked with who claimed to've dug 'em," Windy said, his eyes narrowed in concentration.

"Holes?" Conway asked. "What holes, Windy?"

"Like somebody's been lookin' for somethin' buried that they can't find, Cap'n. 'Nuff holes up there to make a prairie dog feel downright jealous."

"Well, I'll be damned!" Conway exclaimed. "I thought I was on to something, but—"

"She's gone! She's gone!"

Startled, the three of them started to rise in unison, then the door slammed open and Morris burst inside. "She's gone, Captain! Somebody took her!" he gasped. "Lee Ellen, sir! Somebody took her!"

"Nobody could have taken her, Lieutenant. Maybe she tried to take a walk and she's somewhere close by."

"She wouldn't do that, Captain. I told her not to move around, and she wouldn't go against my wishes. The men she said would kill her have come and taken her away. I'm sure of it."

"But how would they—"

"Warner! Lee Ellen's..." Flora's voice trailed off as she ran into the room and saw the four men. "Excuse me, gentlemen, but this is important. Warner, someone's kidnapped Lee Ellen. She's gone. I just stopped by to look in on her and she's gone."

"All right. All right. Just calm down, dear, and you too, Lieutenant. Hysteria will solve nothing," Conway said firmly, rounding his desk to take Flora's hands in his. "You were the last one to see her, weren't you?"

"Yes. I guess I was. Shortly after dark, I stopped in to light her lamp. She was afraid of the dark and I always did that for her. Then, later, about nine o'clock, she was sleeping when I looked in on her, or at least I thought she was, so I just shut the door and left without going in."

"Then she was there at nine o'clock. I'll check with the duty officer who was on last night, but I'm certain that no one came or went after that hour."

"Just a minute, sir. Just a minute," Morris said, sprinting through the orderly room and bounding across the walkway. In seconds he was back with an old blanket clutched in his arms. "This is what was there at nine o'clock, sir. It was arranged in the bed to make it look like someone was sleeping there. That's why it took me so long to find out she was gone. The lamp had gone out, so it was dark in the room and at first I thought it was her and I didn't want to disturb her sleep. Then I looked a little closer after a few minutes and all I found was this damned thing!" he said viciously, throwing the blanket to the floor before glancing at Flora with a reddening face. "I'm sorry, Mrs. Conway. That just slipped out."

"Don't worry about it, Lieutenant. I've heard that and worse before. Who could have taken her, Warner?" Flora asked, her eyes searching her husband's face.

"I don't know, but let's reconstruct the way things were.

150

The photographer's wagon was parked—the photographer!"

"The photographer?" Morris asked.

"Yes, but it's too long a story to go into right now. It had to be him. She couldn't have been taken out of here by any other means than horse or wagon, and on a horse she never would have gotten through the front gate. And the only wagon to come or go yesterday was the photographer's. I thought he was a strange duck, but I was so wrapped up in that telegram that I didn't give him a whole lot of thought."

"What did this feller's wagon look like, Cap'n?" Windy asked softly.

"It was a rather strange contraption actually, Windy. It looked like it had been built especially for his needs. Overly long and high and resembling a rectangular box on wheels."

Kincaid and Mandalian glanced at each other simultaneously. "Are you thinking what I'm thinking, Windy?"

"Sure am, Matt."

Kincaid turned back to Conway. "This morning when we were coming back from the agency, sir, we took the long way around by Pollard Springs, where old Frank Pollard built his place. I thought it would be easier going for the wounded men, even though it was a bit out of our way. We passed by there about five o'clock this morning, and there was a wagon parked there that matches the description you've just given of the one that was here. It was still pretty dark and we didn't think anything of it other than the fact that some travelers had taken shelter in the old Pollard shack for the night. There were four horses tethered there as well."

"Was there any smoke coming out of the chimney?"

"Yes, there was. Again, I just thought they were brewing up some coffee or cooking a little breakfast, maybe."

Conway rubbed a hand across his face in thought. "Let's see now. You came in here about seven o'clock, so that'd make it about an hour and a half's ride, pushing hard, to get back there. You said you saw the wagon and four horses, so that would make it about five men, counting the photographer. Matt? Have two squads mounted and prepared to move out inside of ten minutes. Tell Lieutenant Fitzgerald to lead the patrol and—"

"I'll lead it, sir," Morris said, stepping forward with determination. "I have to lead it, sir. Or at least I have to go along. She might be hurt and I should—"

"No, Lieutenant, you're not going anywhere just now. You're hurt yourself."

"I have to go, sir!"

"You don't have to do anything you're not told to do, mister!" Conway said sharply. "This is an assignment for professional soldiers, not a shot-up doctor. And I don't mean that to impugn your medical skills. If you care for her, either as a person or as a patient, you'll want to see the best men sent to bring her back. You get some sleep. If we do find her, she'll need you more as a wide-awake physician than as a frustrated lover."

"Warner!" Flora said in surprise.

"I mean exactly what I said. I don't blame the lieutenant for being fond of her, if he is, and I believe that to be the case. Therefore, he would be the last person to be sent into a situation where there might be combat involving the individual he is emotionally involved with. Do you understand that, Lieutenant?"

"Yes, sir." Morris replied meekly.

"Good. If she can be returned safely, my men will accomplish that."

"Shall I tag along, Cap'n?" Windy asked. "I've got some personal interest in that little gal myself."

"Thanks, Windy, but no. Send one of the other scouts. You get some rest, too. I want you fresh in case this thing boils up later on."

"Right, Cap'n," Windy replied, ambling toward the door. "Could use a little shut-eye. One of the Delaware will be ready when the squads are."

"I'll have those two squads mounted and out the gate in ten minutes, sir," Kincaid said, following Windy to the door.

Only Morris and Flora remained, and the doctor stooped to pick up the blanket, which he held loosely in his hands in silent contemplation.

After a reasonable wait, Conway asked, "Is there something else on your mind, Lieutenant?"

"Yes. Yes, there is, sir," Morris replied, his head slowly turning toward the commanding officer. "Why weren't there any guards posted outside her door while I was gone?"

"Yes, Warner, why weren't there?" Flora asked in a lowered voice.

"Because," Conway replied slowly and evenly, "I was asked

by a certain doctor and a certain lady, both of whom are standing in this room, to treat her as a patient instead of as a prisoner. I was told by them that they felt it would speed her recovery and give her a chance to prove her innocence. Both of which are still in doubt, I might add."

eleven _____

The soldiers assigned to Easy Company were slowly meandering back from the mess hall, and the midday sun beat down upon Outpost Number Nine with full intensity when the call rang out:

"Patrol comin' in!"

At the shouted words, Kincaid's head jerked up from his pillow and he swung his naked feet over the side of his bunk. His eyes felt like grains of sand had been inserted under their lids as he rubbed them with the heels of his hands and then reached for his trousers and boots. Within two minutes he was dressed and buttoning his tunic as he stepped onto the parade, to be joined by Windy Mandalian, who was still tugging at one boot as he hobbled into the sunlight. Conway stepped from the orderly room and Morris, who obviously hadn't slept, jerked the door open and emerged almost drunkenly from his quarters.

Lieutenant Fitzgerald and Sergeant Breckenridge rode at the head of the two squads as they crossed the parade, and bringing up the rear was the photographer's wagon, with Private Slocum handling the reins. Breckenridge halted the patrol before Conway and saluted smartly.

"They were gone when we got there, sir. From the look of things, they must have been there quite a while. All that was left was that wagon back there and . . . and what's inside."

A look of horror flashed across Morris's face, and he ran toward the back of the wagon and reached for the door handle.

"I don't think you want to look in there, Lieutenant," Breckenridge advised, turning in his saddle. "It's not a real pretty sight."

Morris backed away and Kincaid looked at Conway. "They must have abandoned the wagon, sir. Too easy to track."

"Yes, I suppose so," Conway replied while glancing up at Fitzgerald again. "What's in the wagon, Lieutenant?"

"Maybe you should have a look, sir. It's kind of hard to describe."

Kincaid, Conway, and Mandalian moved toward the back of the wagon in unison, and there was a mutual feeling of dread among them when the scout reached for the latch and opened the door. Lying on the floor, with his face blown away from a bullet fired close up were the remains of G. L. Standish. Five more rounds punctured his massively bloated stomach. The interior of the wagon had been totally destroyed, and what remained of Standish's camera equipment had been strewn over his body. Off to one side, Morris gagged, then bent over at the waist and vomited as he staggered back toward his quarters.

"Is he the photographer you mentioned, Captain?" Kincaid asked in a hushed voice.

"Yes, he is. The magnificent G. L. Standish has taken his last picture, I'm afraid."

"Do you think he was involved in this from the start? The cattle rustling and all that?"

"No, I don't think so. I believe he was a con artist who got conned by some real professionals." He paused, then added, "Professional killers, that is. They must be animals, or at least one of them is. That shot in the face would have killed him; the others were just for pleasure."

"Once you're dead, you're dead, Cap'n, that's a fact. But

whoever did this has got a real bad streak of mean in him," Windy observed, turning to Joseph Hatchet, the Delaware scout who had stayed to the rear of the wagon. "Did you track 'em, Joseph?"

"Yes. There were four horses, and one of them was carrying double, or at least a very, very big man. They knew they would be followed and they stayed to the dry ground and creekbeds. After they left the prairie, we lost their trail."

"That's easy to do around here, Joseph. You did the best you could. Which way were they headed when you lost 'em?"

The Delaware pointed toward the west, and Windy nodded while turning back to Kincaid. "If one of 'em is ridin' double, they won't make it too damned far too fast. And if one of 'em is, that means the woman is still alive. We saw four horses plus this wagon here at the old Pollard place, and the feller who owned this contraption is a worm farm now. Hatchet says they were headed west, so there's not many places they could go to ground with a wounded woman within three days' ride of here."

"No, there aren't, Windy," "Kincaid said. "Captain, I've got a hunch. If everything we've pieced together so far is correct, and if Wes Dobler is actually Weston Doberly, then there is only one place they could go with Miss Dugan. She must have something or know something that they want very badly to take the kind of chances they are, and if they'd already gotten it from her, she would be in the back of the wagon with the poor bastard lying there. It's my guess that they've taken her to Dobler's place. It's due west of here, and close enough so that they could make it fairly easily riding double."

"I believe you're right, Matt," Conway responded without further speculation. "How many men do you want?"

"A full platoon, sir, mounted and ready to move out within the half hour. Maybe we can get to her before they find out what they need to know, but we'll have to move fast, because her life is definitely on the line."

"Take the first platoon. Sergeant Olsen wants a piece of this action himself. The men who killed old Stoney Jenkins are still pretty much on his mind."

"Right, sir. He's a good man, and he doesn't forget an old friend real fast. Windy? Would you find Gus and have him line out his platoon?"

"We'll be ready when you are, Matt," Windy replied, striding away in the direction of the stables.

Kincaid glanced toward the BOQ, where Morris was leaning limply against a post, and asked, "Would you come with me for a moment, Captain? I'd like to talk to the doctor, and I might need your permission for something when I get through."

"Sure, Matt. Lead the way."

"Captain," Lieutenant Fitzgerald asked, "what do you want me to do with that back there?"

"Take the wagon out on the prairie and burn it, Lieutenant. Then have a detail bury Standish's remains."

"Right, sir. One more thing, Captain. I don't know if any of you noticed it or not, but that poor son of a bitch was scalped too."

"No, we didn't, Lieutenant, and thank you for pointing that out. But I don't think scalping implicates the local Indians in this. We're pretty certain who we're after."

Morris looked up as the two officers approached, and he tried to square his shoulders while brushing a fleck of vomit from his chin.

"I'm sorry," he offered in a downcast voice. "I was afraid it might be her. Then when I saw that . . . that *thing,* it was too much of a shock for my stomach to handle. I've seen a lot of cadavers before, sir, but none that looked like that."

Kincaid smiled understandingly. "There's a hell of a lot of difference between a murdered man out here and a cadaver in a city morgue back East, Lieutenant. We've all had the same reaction you've just experienced at one time or another. Forget it, because we have more important matters to deal with right now." He watched the Lieutenant closely. "We think Miss Dugan is still alive."

Morris straightened with a jolt, his jaw dropped partially open, and his eyes filled with renewed hope. "You do? How do you know?"

"I didn't say 'we know.' I said 'we think.' Slater, or one of his men, is riding double, and we believe that indicates she hasn't been killed yet. We're going after her in a few minutes." Kincaid looked at the captain. "I would like to ask your permission to have the doctor accompany us, sir. If Miss Dugan is still alive when we find her, she will have gone through quite an ordeal. It might do her good, both physically and mentally, to have Lieutenant Morris there."

Conway nodded. "I understand and agree completely. Are you capable of going, Lieutenant?"

"Yes, sir," Morris replied firmly. "I want to be there when she's found, one way or the other."

"Good. That's what I had hoped to hear. You have my permission to accompany Lieutenant Kincaid."

"Thank you, sir. But I do have one request."

"What's that, mister?"

"I'd like to be armed, Captain. If it comes to a fight for her, I'd like to do my part."

"Have you ever killed a man before, Lieutenant?"

"No, sir. But I'm prepared to, if necessary."

Conway smiled in appreciation at the tone of commitment in the slim young Lieutenant's voice. "You're made of better stuff than I had thought. Certainly, you can be armed. Matt might need all the fighting men he can get. Draw a weapon from the supply sergeant. With that bad arm of yours, I'd suggest a Scoff over a Springfield."

"A Scoff, sir?" Morris asked. "I'm afraid I'm not too familiar with weapons, Captain. Might I inquire what that is?"

Both Kincaid and Conway chuckled as they turned away. "Just tell him you want a weapon, Doc," Kincaid said. "Skinflint will know what to give you, and I'll show you which end you point at them and which end we'd like to have facing our way."

"What the hell did you bring her here for, goddammit!" Dobler shouted as Slater struggled up the steps with Lee Ellen draped over his shoulder.

"I had to bring her here, Wes. An army patrol came by the shack this mornin' and we had to get the hell out of there. We left the wagon behind 'cause it'd be too easy to follow."

"What'd you do with that photographer you were talking about?"

Dan Reeves grinned as he leaned a hip against the kitchen table. "He's been taken care of, Wes. I handled that little chore personally. Got a little sick of his bullshit after a while. Put enough holes in him to where he wouldn't float in a mud hole."

"Good. Has she talked yet, Jake?"

"No," Slater grunted, carrying Lee Ellen into the bedroom and laying her down. "She's been mostly unconscious since we took her."

Dobler's hand went to his right ear and he stroked the scar with his thumb. "She will. Mark my word on that, she'll talk. She knows where to find what I want, and I've waited ten damned long years to get it. She'll talk, all right."

"Sure she will, Wes. I'm sure of it. Just give her a little time, that's all," Slater urged with almost gentle concern.

"A little time? The one thing we haven't got is time, Jake, you dumb son of a bitch! Do you think the army is just going to sit on its ass and let you waltz away with her? From what you told me about the way she was captured, they have to consider her a prisoner, and in that, and she's probably their only witness against us. They'll be after her, you can bet your ass on that, and they're most likely out looking for her right now."

"Charlie One-Jump took that photographer feller's scalp, Wes," Slater countered meekly. "It was my idea. I thought it might help throw 'em off our trail."

"Shit, Jake! You haven't thought since the last time you wiped your ass, and Christ knows how long that's been. If they found the wagon, they'll know it's the same one they saw at the outpost. It won't take them long to figure out how she was taken out of there, and they'll know for damned sure it wasn't a tribe of goddamned Indians that did it!"

Slater flinched, then tried an uncertain smile. "We hid our trail the best we could, Wes. It won't be easy trackin' us here, that's for damned sure."

"That's the only hope we've got, because it just might buy us a little time." Dobler turned toward the table and angrily splashed whiskey into a dirty tin cup. "Time," he said rhetorically. "Goddamned time. Ten years of waiting and it comes down to this—a few lousy fucking hours. The army has been here before, Toby told me that. He didn't say why, but I'm hoping it had something to do with that contract I have to supply beef to the reservation. As far as I know, they have no reason to suspect me of anything except that Harmon and Bixby were pushing stolen cattle when they got killed." He spun suddenly and his eyes fell on Slater. "You never mentioned my name to that woman back there, did you?"

160

"No, Wes. I never said a word about you. And I don't think she ever talked, either. I told her if she ever got away from me and talked, I'd kill her father and then her."

"Then she still thinks her father's alive?"

"Yeah. I guess so."

"Good. We can use that. Come on, I'm going to wake her up and get some straight answers."

"It won't do no good, Wes. Like I done said, she's passed out."

"She won't be when I get through with her," Dobler snarled, brushing past the big man, who made no attempt to block his way.

Lee Ellen lay flat on her back with her eyes closed, and there was a spot of red on the bandage covering her shoulder, which indicated that the wound had started to bleed again. Dobler walked up and hovered over her for a second before slapping her sharply across one cheek and then the other. Lee Ellen's head snapped from side to side and a trickle of blood ran from the corner of her mouth, which she touched timidly with the tip of her tongue as her eyelids fluttered open. She looked first at Dobler then at Slater, and instead of responding in terror, a look of deep hatred filled her eyes.

"Can you hear me?" Dobler asked brusquely.

"Yes," she replied weakly. "I can hear you."

"Good, because you've got some questions to answer. Your father gave you part of a map, which he said you memorized. I want you to describe exactly what was on that map."

Lee Ellen smiled in cold defiance. "I will tell you nothing."

Dobler's hand shot out again and his palm hit her cheek in a resounding slap. Lee Ellen winced as her head jerked to one side, but she did not cry out in pain or plead for mercy, which infuriated Dobler all the more, and he hit her again.

"Talk, damn you, bitch! Talk!"

"I will," she replied, her eyes locked on his. "You go straight to hell."

Formed into a fist this time, Dobler's hand came back again, and Slater stepped forward to catch his arm just as he started to release the blow. "That ain't gonna do no good, Wes. You could kill her, and that ain't what neither of us wants." He glanced down at Lee Ellen and smiled in a sickly way that was intended to be gentle. "Look, honey, you'd best be tellin' us

161

what we want to know, or we'll kill your daddy."

Lee Ellen watched him coldly. "Where is my father?"

"One of the boys has got him down at the barn. All I gotta do is walk to the front door and wave my arm, and he'll be dead."

"Bring him to me. I want to see him."

"Sorry, honey. I can't do that."

"Why?"

Slater hesitated, trying to think of a plausible reason. Failing, he replied simply, "'Cause I don't want to, that's why."

"I'll tell you why you can't bring him to me," Lee Ellen said sharply, her eyes ablaze with hatred. "Because he's dead. You killed him. If he were alive, you wouldn't need me for this. You would get your information from him. He's dead you . . . you *bastard!* And you killed him!" she screamed.

Dobler nodded his head toward the door that led to the hallway, and jerked his arm free of Slater's grasp. "Come out here. I want to talk to you."

After the door had closed behind them, Dobler turned in a blinding rage. "Now what the hell did you do that for, you ignorant son of a bitch! You played our ace on a bluff hand, and she called your bluff! You're so goddamned dumb you're a menace even to yourself, let alone anyone else who happens to get tangled up with you!"

"Hell, I'm sorry, Wes."

"You're not sorry, Jake. You're stupid!"

A hint of red touched Slater's bristly cheeks, and his piglike eyes narrowed to tiny, puffy slits. "Don't call me that no more, Wes. Don't call me that no more. I'm the one what spent ten years in prison. I'm the one what's done all the shitty work on this deal. Sure, maybe you're the one what's the brains behind it, but that don't make you somethin' special. Don't call me stupid no more."

Listening to the man's voice, Dobler was reminded of a big, ignorant child who was willing to play with kids smaller than him and even be the butt of their jokes, but once they turned cruel, he turned mean. And he knew the only way to play the game was to use intelligence to bend the will of brute strength.

"All right, Jake. I shouldn't have said what I did. We're partners, and we're in this thing together. But we've got to get that woman to talk, and talk now. Since she has figured out that her father is dead, we've got only one other choice." He watched Slater's face muscles relax and asked in a soothing voice, "We are still partners, aren't we, Jake?"

"Sure we are, Wes," Slater replied contritely. "I hope so, anyway. I just got a little mad, that's all."

Dobler headed toward the kitchen, with Slater following. "Entirely understandable. It was my fault. Now, just go outside and cool down a little bit. I've got some thinking to do, and I do that better by myself. Here," Dobler said cordially, picking the bottle up from the kitchen table and handing it across, "take the rest of the whiskey with you. Come back in about half an hour and I'll have a plan."

Slater shrugged his massive shoulders, took the bottle, and shuffled toward the porch door while looking across at Reeves, who still sat with one hip propped on the table. "You comin', Danny?"

Reeves glanced at Dobler and noted the tiny negative shake of his head. "I'll be right behind you, Jake. I want to talk to Wes for a second."

Slater grinned oafishly and shook the bottle. "Don't take too damned long. There ain't much whiskey left in here."

"I won't be long, Jake. Save me a couple of swallows."

"Sure. I'll do that."

After Slater had gone, Reeves crossed to stand beside Dobler. "You sure know how to handle him, Wes. Anybody else, including me, would have killed him long ago."

"Yes, I do. I learned early on in life that you can't drag an ignorant mule nearly as far as you can lead it. The main thing is, I got him out of here. He's too fond of that woman back there to do what has to be done."

"Such as?"

Dobler's face went cold, and the pockmarks on it were like tiny indentations on a frozen rock. "Have you got that fold-up skinning knife in your pocket?"

"Sure do. Sharp as a razor and never without it."

"Good. I've seen you work with it before, and I want your best job now. I'm going to ask her one more time to describe that map for me, and if she refuses again, we're going to do some cutting."

"Where?" Reeves asked, fingering the knife caressingly in his pocket.

"First the left nipple . . . then the right. Let's go."

From where he lay hidden in a stand of cottonwoods, Windy Mandalian made one final search of the sprawling ranch below, then crawled on his stomach to the crest of the rise and slipped down the other side out of sight. The roan stood waiting, and he snatched up the reins and leaped onto his saddle while jerking the horse's head around to race toward the next prairie swell.

An entire platoon of mounted infantrymen waited in a cluster below, the faded blue of their uniforms contrasting with the sea of green grass. Kincaid broke away from the assemblage and rode forward to meet the scout, whose horse was plunging to a stop.

"Did you see the woman?" he asked as Windy controlled his skittish mount.

"No, I didn't see her, Matt. But I'm sure she's there. I just saw Slater walk out of the house with a whiskey bottle in his hand. A big, ugly bastard like him would be kind of hard to miss."

"Have they got any guards posted?"

"One, just up the hill from the house. I'd guess him to be a half-breed. Looks like ten, maybe twelve men standing around down by the bunkhouse."

"Then that leaves at least two inside with Miss Dugan."

"Yup, that's the way I figure it."

"Got any suggestions? An all-out attack would certainly jeopardize her safety."

"No doubt about that, Matt. You said you were inside the house the other day—how's it laid out?"

Kincaid pursed his lips in thought. "Pretty standard, I'd say. There's a main front room where the safe was, and a kitchen in the back and a bedroom or two, I suppose. Since the woman is wounded, I think we would be safe in assuming that she's being kept in one of the bedrooms."

"Yeah, I'd say so. We've got to get a man inside that building before an attack can be made. They seem to be sort of relaxed down there now, and if we move fast we can probably take 'em by surprise."

"Any way that we can slip up to the house from the rear?"

"Not with that breed standin' guard, but I can take care of him. It's gotta be a one-man show, though. Let's have one squad ready to come down from the top and the other two from the sides. Once I get to Lee Ellen, I'll fire three shots, then you close in."

"That's pretty damned risky," Kincaid cautioned. "I'm not too damned fond of the idea of you going down there alone."

"That's what I get my pay for, Matt," Mandalian replied simply. "If there wasn't any risk to this business, everybody and his damned brother'd be doin' it, and I'd be back trappin' beaver again. Give me ten minutes."

"Ten minutes. If I haven't heard your signal by then, I'll attack anyway and hope for the best as far as Miss Dugan is concerned. One more thing, we know Dobler's men have taken the woman supposedly to get some information from her, and we're pretty sure it has to do with the missing bank money. If he makes a break for it, I'm going to try and see if I can't let him slip away. Then, after he gets a decent head start, we'll follow. I'd just as soon find that money now, because some other low-life son of a bitch will sure as hell be coming around here looking for it again sooner or later if we don't."

"Good idea. But if he's in that bedroom with Lee Ellen and I can get a clear shot at him, he won't be goin' nowhere."

"I understand that. Her safety comes first. I'll go back and get my squads lined out. You've got ten minutes, and be damned careful, you hear me?"

"Like a frog croakin' in the moonlight." Windy grinned. "Careful is the only way I work, Matt. You know that."

"Sure I do." Kincaid started to turn his mount away, then stopped and pointed toward the horizon to the north. "Now, who the hell do you suppose that is?"

Mandalian glanced over and studied the rider coming toward them with one hand waving a hat in the air and the other clutching his saddlehorn as his horse moved forward at a painful trot. Windy couldn't help smiling when he realized who it was.

"That's old Roy, Matt. Ridin' like ten pounds of loose flour, just like he always does. Hard to say which one of 'em is gettin' the worst of it, him or the horse."

As the agent drew near, they could see the agonized expression on his face, and when he finally slowed his mount to a stop, he leaned back in the saddle to catch his breath.

"Hello, Roy," Kincaid said. "Judging by the look on your

face, I'd say you're here on business, not pleasure."

"Damned right I'm here on business, Matt," Stearns snapped. "You couldn't get me on top of this old son of a bitch for anything else. I was headed toward the post when I saw you fellers down here."

"What's on your mind? We've kind of got our hands full here right now."

"And you might have 'em full later, too. Kills Many Bear sent one of his trusted braves to the agency this morning with some bad news. He said that Beaver Claw had left the reservation and that he's going after white scalps to avenge the death of his nephew, and besides, his pride's been hurt and he's trying to save face. Kills Many Bear says he's sticking by his word and that his people will not leave the reservation, but if Beaver Claw breaks a promise that affects the entire Sioux tribe, then Kills Many Bear will go after him and we'll have that medicine war we've been tryin' to prevent."

"How many warriors does Beaver Claw have with him, Roy?"

"Don't know. That young buck didn't say and I forgot to ask. He did say something about 'the forbidden hunting ground,' though, 'cause that's where Beaver Claw's nephew was killed, and any whites he finds in that area are fair game for the blood score he feels he's got to settle."

Kincaid and Windy immediately glanced at each other, then Kincaid looked at the agent once more. "We have reason to believe that the man behind all this is Wes Dobler, Roy, and his spread is just over the next rise. He is holding a woman prisoner and we know her life is in jeopardy. Our first responsibility is to try and get her out of there breathing and in one piece. After that, we'll head on up toward the northeast corner of Dobler's property and see if we can head off Beaver Claw before he does something that we'll all be sorry for. In the meantime, you'd better stay with us. If Beaver Claw does go on the warpath, you would be the first whie man he'd come across."

"That's fine with me, Matt. Beaver Claw hasn't ever been real fond of me."

"Yes, I know. You just stay back out of the way once the fighting starts here. Windy? I think we'd better move out now, don't you?"

"I'm gone, Matt. Ten minutes. Have one of your men come up and bring my horse back, 'cause I'll be goin' in on foot."

"Fine. Ten minutes and we'll start the attack."

twelve _____

Lee Ellen watched the two men enter the room, and she knew by Slater's absence that what little protection she had was now gone. She had observed Reeves in the past, and she knew there was something cold and sinister about the otherwise handsome young man—an ever-present deadliness combined with the patient detachment of a rattlesnake about to strike. She had felt him watching her with hungry eyes, and, were it not for Slater, she was well aware that she would have been raped long ago by the man now approaching her. She recoiled against the coarse blankets and tried to squirm as far away as possible.

"Now, Lee Ellen," Reeves said innocently, "you're not afraid of me, are you?"

Her skin went clammy and her eyes were wide with fright

as his hand closed about her thigh. She jerked her leg away with a shudder.

"Later, Danny," Dobler said, while continuing to watch Lee Ellen. "Miss Dugan, you have no choice but to cooperate with us. I wish to see no harm come to you, but please be assured that I will do whatever is necessary to get the information I want. Now I'm going to ask you one last time—what were the details of that map you memorized? The one your father gave you—which belonged to me, by the way, and which you destroyed."

Lee Ellen shook her head in tight little jerks and pulled the blanket up to her chin with one hand.

"I'm trying to be kind, Miss Dugan," Dobler continued, his words firm and the expression on his face one of cold anger, "but I am not a patient man. Describe the map for me in complete detail, and do it now!"

Again, Lee Ellen shook her head. "I . . . I can't remember." she replied weakly.

"You can't remember? Now that is too bad. Perhaps Danny here can help bring your memory back," he said, glancing at the leering young man beside him. "Do you think you could do that for her, Danny?"

Reeves's hand slid into his pocket, and the knife came out with the blade snapping open in one continuous motion. "Just like you suggested in the other room, Wes," he replied.

Dobler's hand shot out and covered Lee Ellen's mouth to seal off her screams while Reeves grabbed the blanket and jerked it away. His fingers went immediately to the bodice of her nightgown, which he ripped from her body with a single, vicious, tearing motion. He looked down at Lee Ellen's firm breasts, which rose and fell with each ragged breath. After running his hand up her flat stomach, he closed his fingers around her left breast and caressed it in obvious pleasure. His eyes had the look of a man in a trance, mesmerized by the sight of a beautiful, naked woman.

"Ain't they beautiful," he whispered in a hoarse voice, incapable of taking his eyes from her. "Have you ever seen a more beautiful set of tits, Wes?"

"Get on with it, Danny," Dobler replied firmly.

The young outlaw slowly took the nipple of Lee Ellen's left breast between his thumb and forefinger, and lifted upward on the firm knob of pinkish flesh, while positioning the knifeblade

170

a mere quarter of an inch away. Razor-sharp metal began to move in a cutting motion, then stopped with Dobler's barked words.

"Hold it, Danny! All right, Miss Dugan, you'd better get your memory back damned quick. First the left nipple and then the right. After that, if I don't get what I want, it'll be the whole tit. Now you wouldn't want that, would you, Miss Dugan?"

Lee Ellen's head shook beneath his hand, and Dobler nodded with a smile.

"No, I didn't think so. I'm going to take my hand away now. If you scream, your nipple is gone. I want you to talk slow and easy, and don't forget the slightest detail." The hand came away and he stared down at her. "I'm waiting, Miss Dugan."

Lee Ellen's terrified eyes were riveted on the knifeblade and she began to talk in a hushed, frightened tone, as if any loud sound might send the blade slicing into her.

"There were two intersecting lines on the map, which came together at a tree, then went off to the right at a forty-five-degree angle. It was a single line after that and the words 'exactly fifty paces' were written beside it. It showed a large boulder, then the line went off at a forty-five-degree angle to the left and stopped at another tree. Again it said, 'exactly fifty paces.' There was an X there with a circle around it, and it showed a hollowed-out place in the trunk of the tree near the bottom. At that point it said, 'Newcastle.' That's all I can remember."

"So that's why I couldn't find it," Dobler said musingly, with a satisfied nod. "The old bastard didn't bury it after all. He hid it in a hollowed-out tree. Thank you, Miss Dugan. Your memory made an amazing comeback."

Reeves's hand had strayed beneath the torn nightgown and was caressing Lee Ellen's pubic mound with smooth strokes while he moved the knife point to her throat, just below the chin.

"She's beautiful, Wes," he said huskily. "Just too damned beautiful to leave here without takin' a little pleasure."

"Do whatever you want, but make it fast," Dobler replied, moving toward the door. "We'll be leaving here, with or without you, just as soon as we can get mounted up."

"It won't take long, Wes. Not long at all, and she's gonna love every minute of it," Reeves said, his eyes glazing over and his hand tugging at his gunbelt. "Don't worry about me, I'll be right behind you."

Dobler shrugged and stepped through the doorway. "Suit youself. But kill her when you're through. She's the only witness the army's got against us."

"I will, Wes. I sure will," Reeves replied as though not having heard Dobler's words, while the gunbelt slipped down his narrow hips.

The half-breed, Charlie One-Jump, had been leaning against a tree with one foot propped behind him, picking his teeth with a sliver of wood, when Windy Mandalian's knife went into his throat just below the right ear. He lurched upward sharply and the rifle slipped from his grasp, and Mandalian guided the half-breed down the tree to slump forward in a sitting position. The scout jerked his knife free, wiped its blade on the dead man's shoulder, then returned it to its sheath while pulling his long-barreled Colt from its holster and springing toward the rear of the building. With his back pressed against the wall, he moved silently toward the sound of voices coming from an open window, and listened to the parting conversation between Reeves and Dobler. When he heard the sound of boots cross the room and fade away along the hallway, he rose up to steal a glance through the corner of the window. Instantly he saw the knife held to Lee Ellen's throat by a tall man leaning over her, working frantically at the buttons of his pants. With one smooth motion, the hammer came back on Windy's Colt and its barrel swung upward while Windy spun to square away before the window. The barrel centered on Reeves's chest as Windy pulled the trigger and the .44-40 cartridge detonated with a flat boom. The slug smashed into Reeves's upper rib cage to slam him against the wall while two more shots in rapid succession ripped into his sagging body. Mandalian was through the window before the reverberation of his shots had died, and a startled Lee Ellen stared up in horror at this new intruder.

Ignoring the girl and the dead man momentarily, Windy crossed to the door and opened it slightly to peer up and down the hall. He could hear shouts from outside and the thudding of running boots. He slammed the door, threw the lock home, then dragged Lee Ellen's bed up against the opposite wall.

"Who . . . who are you?" Lee Ellen asked in a terrified voice, while covering her body with the blankets.

"A friend, little miss," Windy replied, continuing to make preparation for the fusillade of bullets that he knew would soon splinter the door. "Do you remember an old horse named Buster?"

The frightened woman searched her mind. "Yes. Yes, I do. It was a horse I had when I was a little girl, about five, I think. Why?"

"You were exactly five, Lee Ellen. You got it for your birthday. I know because I gave it to you."

Lee Ellen watched him incredulously as he jammed three fresh cartridges into his Colt. "A friend of my dad's gave me that horse. His name was Windy Mandalian. Are you—"

"Yup, I am. You grew up to be just as purty as I thought you would. Stay back against the wall now, as far as you can. I can hear one of 'em runnin' toward the door." Stepping quickly to the other side of the room, Windy positioned himself where he could cover both the door and the window.

There was total silence for several seconds, then an angry voice bellowed from beyond the door, "Reeves? You all right in there? Reeves? Lee Ellen?"

Silence, then a boot slammed against wood, and Windy fired twice through the upper panel of the door. He heard a surprised grunt just before three poorly aimed shots splintered the door, and then there was the solid thud of a lifeless body falling to the floor. Beyond the building, Springfields fired in crashing volleys from both sides, and they could hear startled screams of wounded men and the wild clatter of horses running in several directions.

After waiting possibly a full minute, Windy carefully slid the bolt aside with his back pressed to the wall, then leaped into the dim hallway, swinging his Colt rapidly in one direction, then the other. No target appeared, and he looked down at the man sprawled faceup on the floor. With a bullet in his chest and a second one in his stomach, Slater stared at the ceiling above him with sightless eyes.

Running to the front door in a crouched position, Windy heard the last rounds being fired by those of Dobler's men who had managed to escape. The front yard was littered with the bodies of those who had not. The three squads had advanced on foot, and handlers were now bringing mounts up and soldiers were swinging into saddles while Kincaid and his squad rushed toward the front door.

"It's me, Matt!" Windy said sharply, stepping onto the porch. "We've got two dead ones in here and one more back on the hillside."

"You're not hurt?" Kincaid asked, slowing as he joined the scout on the porch.

"Naw. Did Dobler get away?"

"Yes. Just like we planned. How's Miss Dugan?"

"Scared to death, but other than that, she's just fine."

In his haste, Morris had tripped and fallen, but now he scrambled to his feet and rushed forward with his medical bag in hand. "Is she all right, Windy?" he asked, his face drawn and pale with concern.

"Yes, she's gonna be all right, Doc. She's in that bedroom back there. She's had one hell of a scare, and she just might need a little comfortin' 'bout now. Go on back and look in on her."

"Thanks, Windy," Morris replied, squeezing past the two men and running down the hall.

"Did you see the look on that young feller's face, Matt?" Windy asked with a shake of his head. "Didn't look to me like any doctor runnin' to answer the call of his oath."

"He wasn't," Kincaid replied with a smile. "At least not totally."

"What's your meanin' by that?"

"While we were waiting for your signal, he came up to talk to me. He was really nervous, both about the battle and Miss Dugan's welfare. He asked me to do him a favor if he got killed."

"What was that?"

"To tell her he had planned to ask her to marry him."

Mandalion glanced toward the door and grinned. "He don't look real dead to me. Maybe he can handle that little chore himself."

"Yes, I expect he will, and I wish him well. So much for young love right now, Windy. I'll leave a squad here to protect Morris and Miss Dugan, then after we've given Dobler enough time, we'll go after him. He headed toward the northeast corner of his property."

Mandalian stared in the direction suggested, and slowly pulled his square of cut-plug from a pocket. "If he is, there might not be much to go after if we wait long enough."

"What do you mean by that, Windy?"

The scout cut off a chunk of tobacco and nestled it in his cheek. "What I mean is, if old Roy was right 'bout what he said a while ago, Beaver Claw and his warriors might just do that little job for us themselves." Mandalian spat, then wiped his mouth. "Way I see it, they've got that right."

Wes Dobler glanced over his shoulder one final time, and seeing no pursuing soldiers behind him, he was confident that he had escaped with a sufficient lead to find the money and continue his flight. He concentrated on the directions Lee Ellen had given him, and was certain he had seen that hollowed-out tree before. And now, with his four accomplices either dead or captured, there would be no split to make and the entire fortune would be his. A feeling of satisfaction welled up in him, and his fingers fairly itched to touch those money bags that had eluded his grasp for so long. He wondered briefly if Reeves had managed to rape the woman before that surprise attack by the army, and he envied him if he had. She was indeed beautiful, Dobler allowed, but not worth the price Reeves had paid to have her. Fifty thousand dollars would buy lots of beautiful women and he wouldn't have to hold a knife to their throats to have them.

Nearly three hours had passed before he saw the first of the holes old Toby Brock had dug, and there, just to the left, was where his portion of the map had ended. Slowing his mount, he searched the scattered cottonwoods ahead before dismounting at the one that would have been the intersection point Lee Ellen had mentioned. Then, carefully, he counted out fifty paced steps away to the left at a forty-five-degree angle, changed course to the right for a matching distance, and stopped to run his hand across the bark of a big tree standing before him. His heart raced and his throat was exceedingly dry as he dropped to his knees and began pulling away weeds and moss, which had grown to conceal the hole. Slowly, cautiously, his hand went into the blackness and he could sense the damp coolness as he probed toward the bottom. His fingers touched something that felt like fabric, and he closed his eyes in thanks as his hand encircled the neck of a canvas sack. His fingers were trembling almost uncontrollably as he withdrew the money bag, struggled with the knot, then pulled out a fat wad of thousand-dollar bills tightly packed together and held by a paper sealing strap.

A shriek of joy escaped his lips as he fanned the money before his face, then quickly laid the bundle aside to reach in and take out three more bags. He started to open them for examination, then changed his mind, and clutching the bags to his chest, he hurried toward his horse.

His step faltered at the sound of two words uttered in a deep, guttural voice:

"White man."

Dobler glanced over his shoulder sharply, the toe of his boot caught on an unseen rock, and he sprawled to the ground. The rotted bags broke open upon impact and bundles of money scattered beneath his chest as he scooped them up while regaining his footing. A solitary Indian sat on his mount no more than twenty yards away, with the rifle held in his hands pointing directly at Dobler, who offered a trembling smile.

"You said something to me?"

"I did," Beaver Claw replied. "You are on Sioux land."

Dobler glanced about nervously before stating, "No, friend. No, I'm not. This is my own ground."

"You are wrong. When the white men took our land from us and put us on this reservation, they were very careful to show us the boundaries. The reservation extends to those trees over there."

Dobler's eyes darted toward the trees twenty yards behind him, and he felt a lump rise in his throat. "There must be some mistake," he said, attempting to sound forceful and failing. "I have the survey papers to prove that this is my ground."

"It is Sioux land. You will take nothing from it, in the same way that the Sioux cannot take buffalo from the forbidden hunting ground."

"You can have all the buffalo you want," Dobler offered, his face brightening. "Sure you can. You can hunt here forever if you want—that's fine with me."

"This was not so when the young ones came to hunt. The son of my brother was killed."

Dobler's face reddened, and he tried to feign innocence. "I'm sorry to hear that, friend, but I had nothing to do with it. I give you my word on that."

"*Kah!*" Beaver Claw spat. "The white man's word is like the wind! You have taken our land with this word of yours, and you will take nothing more. Leave what you have in your arms."

Dobler began to back away, clutching the loose bills more tightly to his chest. "I'm going to cross the line onto my side, and if you shoot me there, the army will hang you for the red bastard you are," he snarled. "It's my money and no sonofa-bitchin' Injun like you is going to take it away. There's an army patrol coming this way right now, and—"

The last word froze on his lips, and his eyes went wide with the impact of a bullet tearing through the packets of money held across his chest. He slammed backward to the ground, dead even before his shoulder blades crashed down. The money spilled from his arms and one hand clawed the sky seemingly in search of a bill floating by, carried on a mild breeze.

With no change of expression, Beaver Claw slid from his mount and walked forward. He appeared not to notice the stacks of bills. Laying his rifle down, he pulled his knife from its sheath and deftly stripped Dobler's scalp from his head. Then he rose at the sound of hooves, with the bleeding scalp in one hand and the rifle in the other, and watched the patrol gallop up to stop before him.

Kincaid looked first at the dead man, and then at the medicine chief. "Where are your people, Beaver Claw? I was told that you had brought your warriors to make war on white settlers and Kills Many Bear as well."

"I have come alone," the chief replied. "There is no way I could win against either you or him. He is right. For the sake of our people, we must live in peace. But this one," he said, nudging Dobler with his toe, "would not let us live in peace. I have done what I must do and I will take up the war club no more."

"That's quite a change of heart from the last time I talked with you, Beaver Claw," Kincaid replied. "If I remember rightly, you were ready to make war then."

"I was. But it was I who was the fool, not Kills Many Bear. His son is well, and the white man's medicine saved him when I could not. I ask only what we were promised, and I will live in peace. The death of my brother's son has been repaid, but it was a thing for me to do alone. It is done. I have talked with Kills Many Bear. My people should not be punished for a thing I do myself."

"Can I talk to you alone for a second, Matt?" Windy asked, scratching the back of his head in thought.

"Sure, Windy," Kincaid replied, stepping down and walking

a short distance away, with Mandalian at his side. "What's on your mind?"

"Just an idea. By killing Dobler and taking his scalp, Beaver Claw has regained his face with his people. Face lost by that operation we did. Now, near as I can tell, Dobler was killed on Sioux ground, and accordin' to the terms of the treaty, anything on the reservation when it was laid out is for the Sioux to keep. That includes that money back there, the way I see it. Dobler was stealing from them, and he was killed for his trouble."

Kincaid walked in silence for a few more steps before saying, "Yes, I was thinking along those lines myself. Everybody who was involved in this thing against the Sioux is dead, and we'll be able to supply them with the beef the government promised. I don't know about that money, but you're right, it does belong to the Sioux, according to the terms of the agreement. We'll have to check with the captain, but maybe it could be put into some sort of a trust at the agency for Stearns to use as a fund to buy things they need. And besides, nobody knows for sure where that money came from. After ten years, I think it legally goes to whoever finds it."

"Well, the man that found it ain't going to be needing it, that's for sure. And the man that found it second, Beaver Claw, ain't even touched it yet. Let's scoop it up and leave the decision up to the cap'n."

"Yes, that's the best thing to do, but I think he'll agree with us that it rightfully belongs to the Sioux," Kincaid said, turning back and walking up to stand before Beaver Claw.

The chief's chest swelled, and he threw his shoulders back as if expecting a blow while his expressionless eyes held on Kincaid.

"You are free to go, Beaver Claw," Kincaid said simply. "There will be peace between us and your people, and I'm glad the medicine war between you and Kills Many Bear is over. Go in peace."

Beaver Claw hesitated before nodding. He glanced down at the scalp dangling from his hand, then tossed it aside and, walking quickly to his pony, leaped to its back and galloped away.

Kincaid and Mandalian watched the chief depart before turning away, and the scout knelt beside Dobler while Kincaid began stuffing the money into his saddlebags.

"Just between you and me, Matt, I think we know which bank that money came from," Mandalian said.

Turning, Kincaid glanced down. "Is that right? How?"

Mandalian smiled and touched the hair remaining on the right side of Dobler's head. "Remember when the cap'n found out about that robbery at Newcastle? The man who they suspected might have been the mastermind was a teller with half his right ear missin'?"

"Yes, I remember. What about it?"

Mandalian lifted the straight black hair and pointed at the mutilated ear. "Looks like they had it figured pretty close." Then he grinned. "Or was it Weston Doberly that had half his *left* ear missin', and Wes Dobler who'd lost half the *right* one?"

"Hard to tell," Kincaid replied with a grin. "Maybe the captain can figure that out. Let's go home, partner."

"Yeah, let's do that," Windy replied, swinging up onto his saddle. "First time I've seen my goddaughter in eighteen years, and I ain't said ten civil words to her yet."

RIDE THE HIGH PLAINS WITH THE ROUGH-AND-TUMBLE INFANTRYMEN OF OUTPOST NINE—IN JOHN WESLEY HOWARD'S EASY COMPANY SERIES!

Bestselling Books for Today's Reader — From Jove!